SPHDZ
4 Life!

Sizzlin' Cinnamon Added by
Steven Weinberg

headz

by Jon Scieszka

Extra-Hot Flavor by
Casey Scieszka

Illustrated by
Shane Prigmore

Simon & Schuster Books for Young Readers
New York London Toronto Sydney New Delhi SPHDZ

SIMON & SCHUS[illegible]
BO[illegible]S FOR [illegible]
An [illegible]
Ch[illegible]'s Publish[illegible]
12[illegible]
Ne[illegible] York, [illegible]

The Library of Congress [illegible] the hardc[illegible] edition as follows:
Scieszka, Jon.
SPHDZ 4 Life! / by Jon S[illegible] Prigmore ; [illegible] extra-ho[illegible]ka ; sizzlin' [illegible] added b[illegible] pages [illegible]
Summ[illegible] graduation fast [illegible] to find the missing [illegible] uses it to destroy a planet?
[illegible]-1-4169-7957-9 (hardcover : alk. paper)
[illegible]7958-6 (pbk. : alk. paper)
[illegible] (eBook) [1. Extraterrest[illegible] washing—Fi[illegible]. 3. Schools—Fic[illegible]. 4. Spies—Fiction. 5. Friend[illegible] family life—New York [illegible]—Fiction. 7. Brooklyn (New York, N.Y.)—Fiction.] I. Scieszka, Casey. II. [illegible]le.
[illegible]23
[illegible]

To ALL-NATURA

A FULL-COLOR

—J.

To Elaine and Gia . . . ULTR

—S.

SIMON & SCHUSTER
BOOKS FOR YOUNG READERS
An imprint of Simon & Schuster
Children's Publishing Division
1230 Avenue of the Americas,
New York, New York 10020

Also available in a Simon & Schuster Books for Young Readers hardcover edition
Book design by Dan Potash
The text for this book is set in Joppa.
The illustrations for this book are rendered digitally.
Manufactured in the United States of America
0813 OFF
First Simon & Schuster Books for Young Readers paperback edition October 2013
1 2 3 4 5 6 7 8 9 10

The Library of Congress has cataloged the hardcover edition as follows:
Scieszka, Jon.
SPHDZ 4 Life! / by Jon Scieszka ; illustrated by Shane Prigmore ;
extra-hot flavor by Casey Scieszka ; sizzlin' cinnamon added by Steven Weinberg. — First edition.
pages cm. — (Spaceheadz)
Summary: With a mysterious new principal and fifth-grade graduation fast approaching, will Michael K. and his friends be able to find the missing Brainwave before the chief of the Anti-Alien Agency uses it to destroy a planet?
ISBN 978-1-4169-7957-9 (hardcover : alk. paper)
ISBN 978-1-4169-7958-6 (pbk. : alk. paper)
ISBN 978-1-4424-1297-2 (eBook) [1. Extraterrestrial beings—Fiction. 2. Brainwashing—Fiction. 3. Schools—Fiction. 4. Spies—Fiction. 5. Friendship—Fiction. 6. Family life—New York (State)—New York—Fiction. 7. Brooklyn (New York, N.Y.)—Fiction.] I. Scieszka, Casey. II. Weinberg, Steven. III. Title.
PZ7.S41267Snp 2013
[Fic]—dc23
2012040116

To ALL-NATURAL SOLID-GOLD Shane!

A FULL-COLOR **SPHDZ** *4 Life!*

—J. S.

To Elaine and Gia . . . ULTRA STRENGTH! EXTRA SWEET!

—S. P.

Bzzzzzz

∫ΩΩΩΩΩΩ

Spring bloomed beautiful in Brooklyn.

Flowers unfolded.

Bees buzzed.

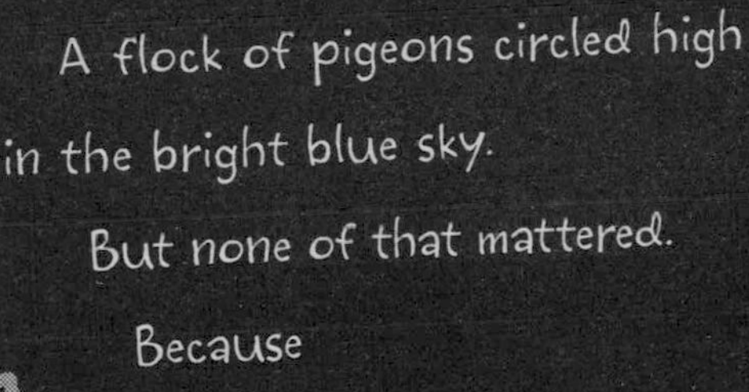

A flock of pigeons circled high in the bright blue sky.

But none of that mattered.

Because

1. the chief of the AAA had turned out to be a bad Spaceheadz in disguise!
2. the chief had stolen the Spaceheadz Brainwave!
3. the chief was going to bllrrp the planet Gonf!
4. the chief was sure to turn off Earth!

And now the only group that could stop him was down to its last plan.

Michael K./his friends Venus and TJ/Spaceheadz Bob, Jennifer, and Major Fluffy/DarkWave X agents Delta, Echo, and Foxtrot/Mom K., Dad K., and Baby K./AAA agents Hot Magenta and Umber sat around the table inside Spaceheadz HQ.

The flickering light of the Spaceheadz TVs lit their very serious faces.

"We've tried everything," said DarkWave X agent Delta.

"We are beat," said Dad K.

"So not ***LEMON FRESH***," said Bob.

"Eeeek eeee eeee," said Major Fluffy.

"Gooo goo gah," agreed Baby K.

Michael K. stood up at the head of the table. "We have to take back our Brainwave and save the world. We are not beat yet."

Everyone around the table grumbled.

"We have ***ALL NATURAL*** failed our SPHDZ assignment," said Jennifer.

"We are ***FAT FREE*** SPHDZ disgrace," said Bob.

The Spaceheadz HQ TV screens flashed a checkerboard of commercials showing steaming tacos, value-menu cheeseburgers, extra-cheesy cheese puffs, hot chunky salsa, and red-hot potato chips.

"We've tried everything," said TJ. "What else can we do?"

"Week eeek eee eeek eee," Major Fluffy suggested. "Squee eeek eek eeee eek eek eee eee."

Great idea," said Venus.

"What's a great idea?" asked Delta.

"Week eeek eee eeek eee," Major Fluffy repeated.

"I don't speak Hamster," said Delta.

"Woof woof bark bark slobber sniff?"

"Or Dog."

"Goo gar goo goo?"

"Or Baby."

Venus typed Major Fluffy's ideas into the translator on fluffysblog.com. "Major Fluffy says he has made a PowerPoint of all of the plans we've tried so far," Venus said, reading her screen. "And he thinks we should watch it and see if we can think of anything we haven't tried."

"That is a great idea," said Michael K.

"Major Fluffy—you handle the laptop," said Venus. "I'll do the talking."

"Eeeee," said Major Fluffy. He hopped on Venus's computer.

A bright white square flashed on the Spaceheadz HQ wall.

Fluffy clicked on the first PowerPoint slide.

PLAN A

π¬å~ å

"Plan A seemed like a good one," said Venus. "Team DarkWave X blasted AAA HQ and the chief with their IWANT Pulsar."

Michael K. nodded. "It should have made the chief want Purple Nertz, a tastier taste snack, and want to give us back the Brainwave.

"Too bad the chief bounced the wave back at them, and doubled its power."

"I really do want some Purple Nertz," said Delta.

"Me too," said Echo.

"Me too," said Foxtrot.

Fluffy clicked a new slide. Venus continued.

"But the worst part was—the chief used the double-strength WantWaves to make DarkWave X want to give the Pulsar to the chief. So they did. And now the chief has the IWANT Pulsar, too."

Agent Delta shook his head.

"Sorry. We couldn't help ourselves. We just wanted to so bad."

PLAN B

π¬å˜ ß

Then Mom K. and Dad K. launched Plan B," said Venus.

"***ATOMIC SMACKDOWN!***" cheered Jennifer.

"Well . . . sort of," said Venus. "At least, that was the idea. Mom K. wrote five hundred and thirty-seven top secret reports to the president, the vice president, the one hundred senators in all fifty states, and the four hundred thirty-five state representatives in Congress.

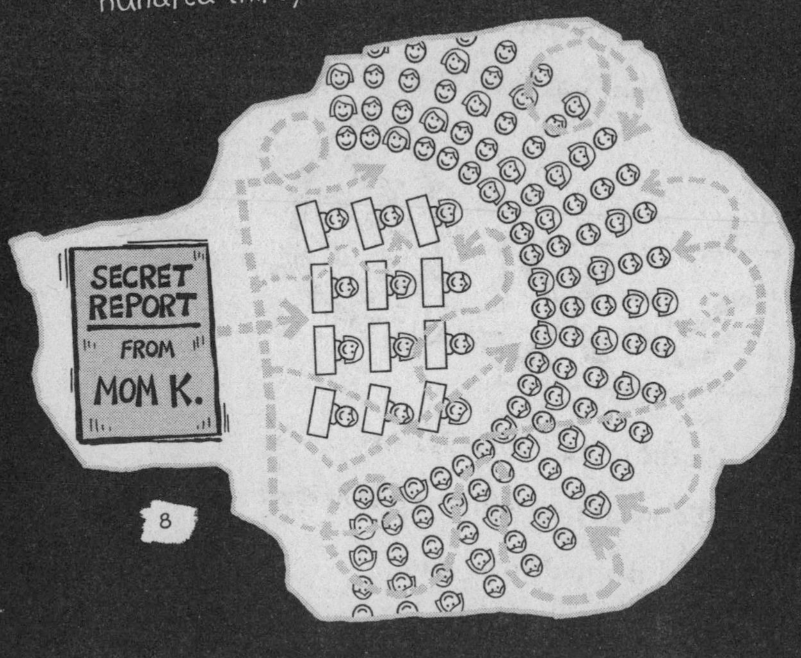

"Dad K. cranked out ads and billboards warning that the chief was evil."

"STARS AND STRIPES FOREVER!" said Bob.

"Yeah," said Venus. "But too bad the chief had already sent out his own reports that Mom K. was not a real American.

"And too bad the chief changed all the billboards."

PLAN C

π¬å˜ Ç

And then Agent Hot Magenta had a brilliant Plan C for a digital attack.

"Which got instantly hacked."

Which was followed by Agent Umber's . . . uh . . . interesting Plan D."

"Maybe not your best AAA disguise," said Agent Hot Magenta.

PLANS E,F,G,H,I,J,K,L, M,N,O,P,Q,R,S,T,U,V,W,X,Y π¬ å˜ß ´≤ ƒ≤ ©≤ ˙≤ ˆ≤ ∆≤ ˚≤ ¬≤ µ≤ ˜≤ ø≤ π≤ œ≤ ®≤ ß≤ †≤ ¨≤ √≤ ∑≤ ≈≤ ¥

Which was followed by plans E to Y:

"E. My Little Pony army

F. Giant squirt gun

G. Ultimate Fighters

H. Time travel

I. Trick glasses

J. Skateboard attack

K. Spy monkeys

L. Make-you-puke pizza

M. Dressed-up kittens

N. Wrestlers

O. Mind control

P. Giant pie in the face

Q. Terrible song that gets stuck in the chief's head

R. Jelly beans that look good but taste like turnips

S. Vikings

T. Cherry bananas

U. Dentists

V. Robots

W. Killer bees

X. Friendly sharks

Y. Origami paper cuts

"But none of those plans worked," said Venus in conclusion.

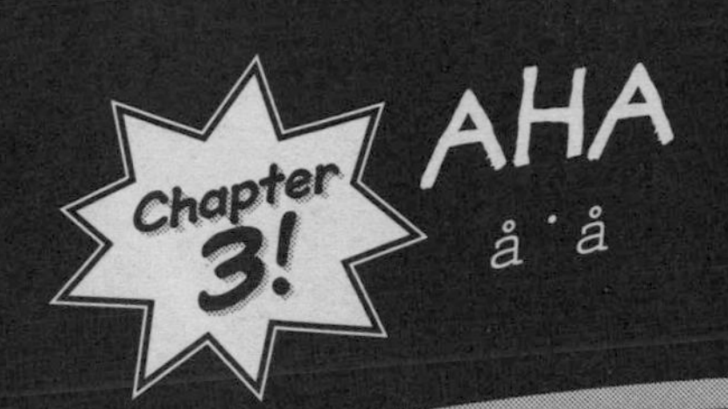

AHA

å˙å

And that is why both Hot Magenta and Umber are now hiding from everyone in their excellent disguises . . ."

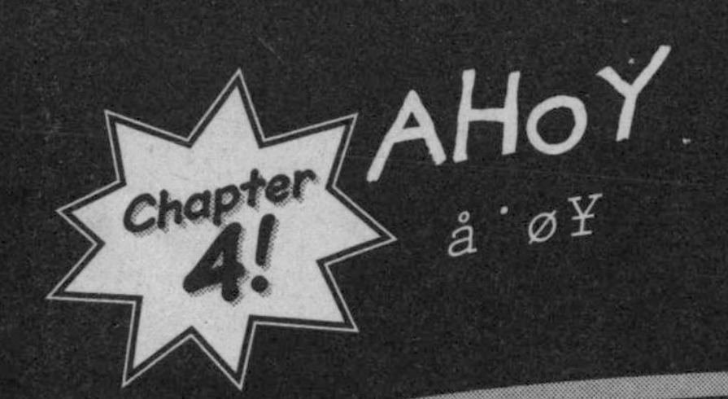

Why DarkWave X is hiding from everyone in their extra-excellent disguises . . ."

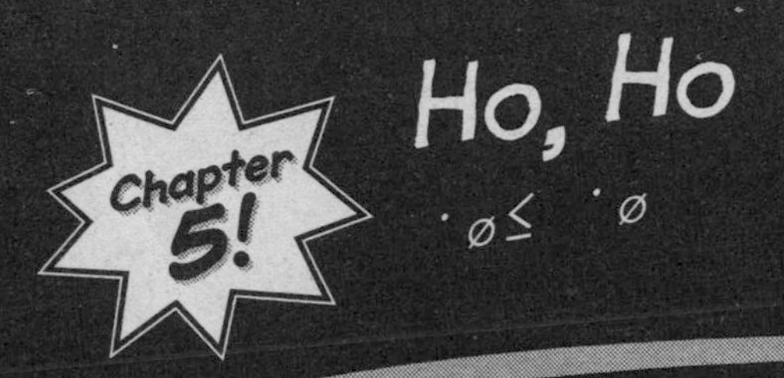

And why Mom K., Dad K., and Baby K. are hiding from everyone in their extra-extra-excellent disguises . . ."

And why we are now all sitting here, stuck with this one giant question:

"Why hasn't the chief used the Brainwave yet?"

"Wow," said Michael K. "That really is a giant question."

Circle I

One definition of a circle is

a group of points, on the same plane,

that are all the same distance

from a fixed center point.

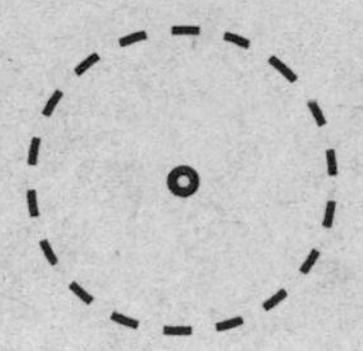

A circle of friends is

a group of people, who are all friends,

often around a center.

Coming full circle is

ending up in the same place you started.

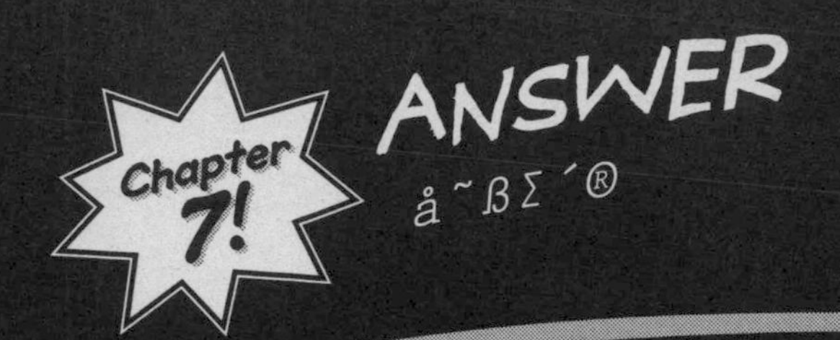

Five Months Earlier
Chief's Office
AAA HQ

Ha!" yelled the chief in his high, squeaky voice. "Finally!"

The chief held up a small snow globe filled with tiny flashing blue lightning bolts.

The chief spun his big AAA office chair in happy circles.

The chief dialed ºº¡-¶¡•-¢∞§-ª•¶§-¡ª• §∞™¢™-¶∞∞¢¡ ™∞•ª• on his coffeemaker's control pad.

"Beep," beeped the coffeemaker. "Medium roast brewing. This is General Accounting."

A cartoon character of a little general popped up on the chief's AAA screen.

"Hello, General. Chief here. We are ready to blast the Brainwave!"

"Rrrrrr," said the coffeemaker. "You tricked everyone. You are very bad guy."

"Yes I am!" said the chief. "Just like you."

The chief hopped out of his AAA office chair. He locked the sparking Brainwave globe into a very red, very nasty-looking Red-Hot Ray.

The chief flipped the power switch on. The Red-Hot Ray hummed. The chief swung the red target sight over the image of Planet Gonf.

"Mmmmmm," said the chief. "First Gonf. Then Earth. Then the uuuuuuuuuniverse! Watch this!"

The chief grabbed the firing handles with both hands.

He counted down out loud, "Five, four, three, two . . . ONE!" and pulled the Red-Hot Ray triggers.

The Spaceheadz Brainwave globe sparked and swirled.

The target sight flashed an even hotter red.

The Red-Hot Ray BZZZZZZRTTTTTed and . . .

Nothing.

The chief pulled the triggers again.

Still nothing.

Again, again, again, again.

Nothing, nothing, nothing, nothing.

"Beep," said the coffee machine. "What is problem? Gonf looks same."

"Arrrrr!" said the chief. "Something is wrong. I'm not getting full power." He smacked the Brainwave globe to make sure it was in place.

It was.

The chief smacked the side of the Red-Hot Ray.

A small black-and-white message popped up on-screen.

ERROR 3.14 – 1

"What?"

The chief clicked on the error message. A further explanation popped up:

Incomplete Brainwave power.

Missing brain wave #1.

"No!" said the chief. "This can't be!"

"PSSSSSSSSSSSSS," hissed the coffee machine in a jet of steam. "Not good news, Chief. If you are mess this up again, you are staying on Earth planet forever."

"Wait, wait, wait," said the chief. "I have the Brainwave. I will show you."

The chief walked to the computer and logged on to www.spaceheadz.com/sphdz-admin.

He watched the Spaceheadz counter hit 3,140,001.

He watched the on-screen fireworks and listened to the cheers.

He watched his moment of triumph as the Brainwave counter spun backward and broke.

And then he saw it.

"That can't be!" said the chief.

But it not only could be, it was.

The Spaceheadz counter, broken in half, still showed "1."

The one missing brain wave that the chief did not have.

"No, no, no, no, no, no!" yelled the chief, pounding his desk and turning beet-red mad.

The images on his computer screen bent and swirled and changed colors. The hands of the clock on the wall whizzed around like an airplane propeller.

The chief stared at the spaceheadz.com screen, still fuming.

"I can't use the Brainwave until I have the whole three point one four million and one. I have to find that missing one."

"You better," said the coffee machine, and it powered off.

"Grrrrrrrr," the chief growled at his coffee machine. He was not happy.

"Bing-bong," chimed the chief's AAA HQ phone.

"What?" said the chief.

"AAA security, Chief. We are being attacked by an army of My Little Ponies."

"Oh, great," said the chief. "Just what I don't need."

"And it looks like there is also a giant squirt gun pointed at us."

"Grrrrrrrr," fumed a very mad chief. "Grrrrrrrrrr."

BACK TO RIGHT NOW

∫åç˚ tø ®ˆ©˙† ˜øΣ

Five Months Later
Chief's Office
AAA HQ

The chief paced back and forth in a darkened room.

"Beep," beeped the coffeemaker. "Extra-dark roast. This is General Accounting."

A cartoon character of a little general popped up on the chief's AAA screen.

"It is been five Earth months since you were going to fix Brainwave and Red-Hot Ray. Why is happening down there?" said cartoon General Accounting. "All reports from you are craziness."

"Tell me about it!" said the chief. "This kid and his annoying SPHDZ friends have been driving me crazy with their attacks!"

"Dressed-up kittens?" asked General Accounting.

"Awful," said the chief.

"A giant pie in the face?"

"Weeks of cleanup," answered the chief.

"PSSSSSSSSSSS," hissed the coffee machine. "Time is no more, Chief. You must fire Brainwave now . . . or you are there left as Earth person. Have you found missing brain wave number one?"

The chief grabbed on to the screen like a man grabbing the last life preserver on a sinking boat.

"I'm on it, General. It's that kid, Michael K. He was the first one to sign up. He must have a special brain wave. It resists wanting. That's why it didn't load."

"Rrrr, rrrr, rrrrrrr," said the coffee machine, grinding. "No more excuses. You have only last chance to get whole Brainwave and bllrrp Gonf!"

"Oh, I have a plan," said the chief.

The chief patted a giant crate next to his desk.

"First I get some pesky people out of the way. . . ."

The chief sat down at his desk. He pushed three red buttons. On the giant world map three red dots started blinking.

"And then I get that one special brain wave."

"PSSSSSSSSSSS," said the coffee machine.

"And please to remember most important All-Earth Warning Number One Big-Time."

"I know. I know," said the chief.

"You know," said the General Accounting coffee machine. "You must never πø˚ ß†ˆç˚ ˆ˜ †¨ å˜†®˜¨†≤ µå˚ µå∂ †¨ ∑ø®¬∂ ∑ˆ∂ ∑˙å¬≤ ø® ©† ¬¬π˙ å˜† ß†å®†∂≥ †˙øß ˜¨†∑ø®˚ß are only force that can ß†øπå three point one four million plus one Brainwave."

"Don't worry," said the chief. "The Earth kid will never figure that out."

The coffee machine gave one last ***PSSSSSS*** and turned off.

The chief ate the last of a red pencil.

Now he knew this really was his last chance.

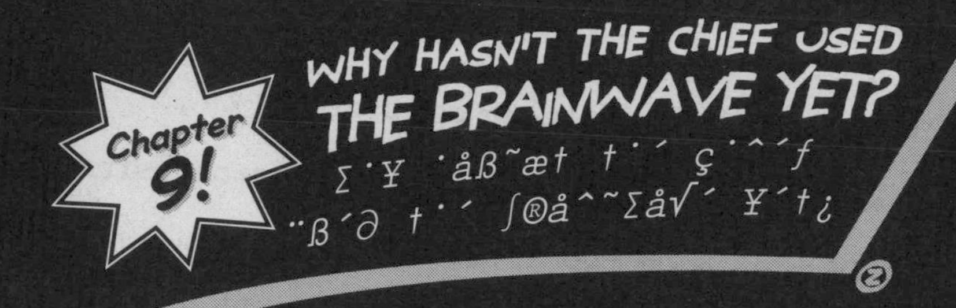

Chapter 9! Why Hasn't the Chief Used the Brainwave Yet?

Σ˙¥ ˙åß˜æ† †˙´ ç˙ˆ´ƒ ¨ß´∂ †˙´ ∫®åˆ˜Σå√´ ¥´†¿

"Why?" repeated Michael K. "I have no idea. But he must be missing something important. Otherwise he would have bllrrped Gonf for sure by now."

"So what do we do?" asked Mom K.

Michael K. smacked his hand on the table. "We capture the chief and take our Brainwave back!"

"Yes!" said Agent Umber, jumping up from his seat.

Venus checked her laptop. "But there is one small problem. After Plan Y the chief disappeared. We have no idea where he is."

"He could be anywhere," said DarkWave X agent Foxtrot.

Everyone looked up at the Spaceheadz world map.

"But where do we even start?" said Agent Foxtrot.

Three spots started blinking on the world map.

"Whoa," said Venus. "Check it out. There is our answer. We just got three Code Red reports. Alaska, Florida, the Amazon."

"Yes!" said Michael K. "The chief has got to be at one of those spots."

"How do we know?" asked Umber.

"Venus and I built this thing to gather all incoming Spaceheadz reports," said Agent Hot Magenta. "Code Yellow is a strong report grouping. Code Orange is a very strong report. And Code Red is almost for sure."

"Then let's roll," said Agent Delta.

Circle II

The distance around a circle is called the circumference ***(***C***).***

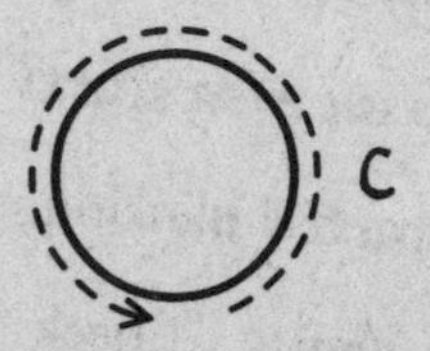

The distance across a circle through its center point is called its diameter ***(***d***).***

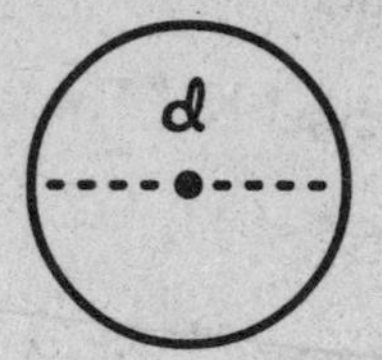

A circle's circumference divided by its diameter is a number called pi. The symbol for pi is the Greek letter π.

$$C/d = \pi$$

The value of π is always 3.14.

It's the same for every circle.

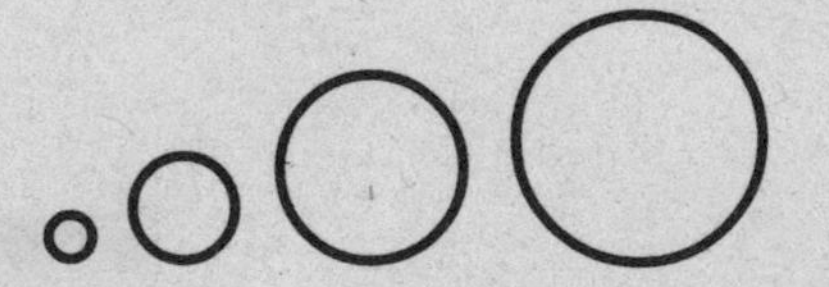

The Spaceheadz team was instantly reenergized. Everyone jumped into action.

"We'll take the Alaska lead," said DarkWave X agent Delta. "We are perfectly disguised for seagoing adventures."

"Agent Umber and I will handle the Amazon alert," said Agent Hot Magenta. "We will use our scientific explorer disguises."

"Are there many bugs in the Amazon?" asked Umber.

"Yes, millions," said agent Hot Magenta. "Good thinking. We will be entomologists, bug scientists. Or better yet—ant scientists! Myrmecologists!"

"Oh, no," said Umber. "I don't like bugs. And I *really* don't like ants."

"Our circus disguises will be perfect for Florida," said Mom K.

"Right," said Dad K. "We will blend in beautifully."

"Gooo gahr gaaah gaaah," said Baby K., which would have saved everyone all kinds of trouble if anyone had listened to her.

Too bad no one understood Baby.

"Eeek weeee eeee eeee," said Major Fluffy.

Except Major Fluffy.

"Hey, wait," said Michael K. "What about us?"

"Yes," said Venus. "We studied all of those places this year in geography."

"North to the Future!" said Bob. "That's the Alaska state motto."

"The Sunshine State!" said Jennifer. "That is Florida's nickname."

"You will be doing the most important job," said Dad K.

"Oh, no," said Michael K. Because Michael K. had heard this sentence before. And it was never followed by anything very important. Or fun.

Dad K. continued, "You and Venus and TJ and Bob and Jennifer will be finishing the school year. So your job will be to stay here and coordinate operations . . . and graduate from fifth grade."

"Oh, man," said Michael K. "That's not important. That's the most boring job ever! The world is about to end, and you want us to go to school?"

"Oh, but a good education is important," said Mom K. "Even at the end of the world."

Everyone stopped to think about that for a minute.

"Well, anyway . . . ," said Hot Magenta. "You will at least be safe at school. We have cleared the whole area of alien activity."

"And you will be our HQ," said Delta.

"Great," said Michael K., not thinking *Great* at all.

* * *

The rest of the teams got ready to brave the chill ocean waters of Alaska, and trek through the Amazon rain forest, and clown around in Florida.

Michael K. and his pals got ready, as usual, to go to school.

"Yes, school is very important," said Dad K., adjusting his clown nose as he hauled his overstuffed clown suitcase out the door. "And sometimes very exciting!"

"Very exciting!" said Bob, really meaning it.

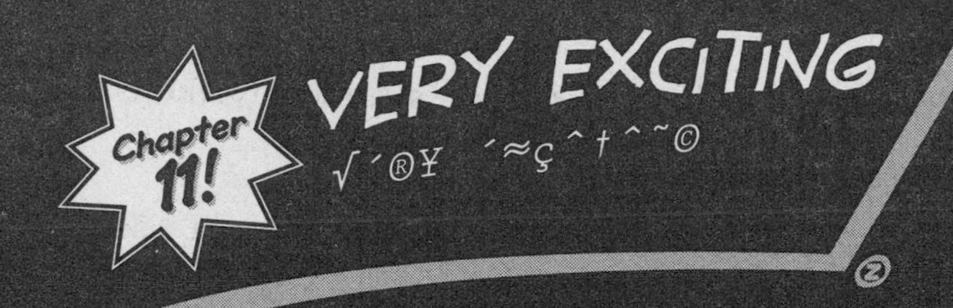

Chapter 11! VERY EXCITING

√´®¥ ´≈ç^†^~©

"U-N-C-O-N-S-C-I-O-U-S," said Mrs. Halley very slowly, with exaggerated emphasis. "Spelling word number seven is 'U-N-C-O-N-S-C-I-O-U-S.' Can someone use spelling word number seven in a sentence?"

"Oh, no," groaned Venus, dropping her head down on her notebook. "These spelling words are boring me unconscious."

TJ was already asleep, with his head on his desk.

Major Fluffy was curled up next to his half-chewed toilet paper tube, snoring.

Bob nodded in his chair. "Why does my brain feel like ***J-E-L-L-O***?"

"It's because your unused brain is turning to mush," said Venus.

Jennifer blinked and started to shake. "Mush? Like pudding? SPHDZ do NOT like mush."

Michael K. remembered what happened the last time Jennifer got upset by pudding. And he did not want to see that again. Michael K. raised his hand.

"Yes, Michael K.," said Mrs. Halley.

"Jennifer is having a bad reaction to spelling practice. And it's almost the end of our fifth-grade year. Do you think we could do something a little more . . . um . . . exciting?"

Mrs. Halley put her finger to her lips and thought for a minute. "Yes," she said. "That is a very good idea. Let's put away our spelling notebooks."

The whole class woke up a bit.

It suddenly looked like a very nice spring day again.

Michael K. smiled.

Mrs. Halley dug inside her desk. "Let's get to the real important and exciting stuff." Mrs. Halley pulled out another notebook. "And let's all take out our math notebooks for . . ."

"Oh, no," said Michael K.

Mrs. Halley held up her math notebook triumphantly. "Adding and subtracting . . . fractions!"

Mrs. Halley loved spelling.

But she really loved fractions.

No one knew why.

The whole room 501-B gave a giant groan like they had been punched in one giant class stomach.

The day had just gone from very boring to painfully boring.

Big Joey shot Michael K. a mean look.

"Thanks for nothing, smart guy."

"Yes, yes, yes," said Mrs. Halley, barely able to contain her excitement. "As you remember, when adding or subtracting fractions, you must first do what?"

"Convert to common denominators," said Michael K. He figured it was the least he could do to help the class out of this mess he had gotten them into.

"Yes!" exclaimed Mrs. Halley, with way more enthusiasm than is ever necessary for fractions.

Venus secretly opened her laptop and started scanning for Spaceheadz network news from Alaska, Florida, or the Amazon.

"So we add one fourth to one third . . ."

All of the teams had landed safely at their destinations. They were closing in on the chief.

Venus showed Michael K. the update.

Everyone else was actually doing something.

"By realizing that twelve is the LCD or least common denominator of three and four. . . ."

Jennifer started to nod off.

"Brain going fuzzy again," Bob mumbled.

"BEEEEEEEEEEEEEEEEEEEEEEP," interrupted the speaker above the door. "This is a special announcement from the principal's office. There has been an unfortunate accident."

"Oh, dear," said Mrs. Halley.

"Principal Edison has been called away," said the voice from the speaker. "Our new principal has asked that everyone stand by for a special graduation assignment."

"Could this year get any weirder?" said Michael K.

"Especially the fifth grade," said the speaker.

"Eeeeeee," said Major Fluffy.

Mrs. Halley handed out the single sheets of paper from the principal's office.

Everyone in room 501-B started complaining.

"Oh, no. Not more homework."

"Who does this new principal think he is?"

"This new principal is terrible!"

"I hate this new principal!"

Then everyone read the assignment.

Assignment

• Examine 2 hours of television tonight.

Must include:

1 cartoon

1 reality show

1 preschool show

64 commercials

• Complete 1 hour of computer activities.

Activities must include:

Video search for "cute animals," "sharks," and "volcanoes"

Visit 12 different websites

Click on 28 different logos

Click 6 agree boxes

• Play 1 hour of video games.

Games must include:

Racing

Jumping over things trying to smash you

Eating things

Smashing and blowing things up

Venus looked up from her sheet. "I think I love this new principal!"

Michael K. looked over the assignment again to make sure it said what he thought it said. "This is crazy. Crazy great. Our new principal is the best."

"**KNOCKDOWN 100% NEW AND DELICIOUS!**" said Jennifer.

"Cool," said TJ. "Maybe we did get the best assignment. This is my kind of graduation work."

Mrs. Halley didn't know what to say.

This was not spelling or fractions.

Mrs. Halley read the assignment again and shook her head.

Goo.

"Goo goo.

"Goo goo gah gah?" asked Baby K.

"Breeeeeee! Eeeeeeee!" answered the circus elephant just outside the tent.

The long, thin, brightly colored circus pennants flapped in the hot and humid Florida breeze.

"We are looking for a little man with a bald head and a squeaky voice," said Mom K. to the circus strong man.

"Oh, yeah," said the giant muscled guy. "That's our head clown. He makes everyone call him Chief."

"Yes!" said Dad K., tying the yellow laces on his giant green clown shoes. "It must be him. Where is he?"

"He only does the big-top show tomorrow," said the strong man.

"Okay," said Dad K. to Mom K. and Baby K. "We will blend in with the other clowns. Act natural. Act funny. Then we make our move and grab the chief!"

"Goo gah," warned Baby K., shaking the giant frilly bonnet on her head.

"Breee beee beee," suggested Ella the elephant.

"Ding-ding-ding-ding," rang the tiny clown fire truck bell.

Dad K., Mom K., and Baby K. climbed into the very small red truck to clown around.

A cold blue wave slapped the gunmetal gray hull of the DarkWave X stealth boat.

Giant cliffs of white-blue ice towered over the tiny craft bobbing in the rough chop.

Foxtrot braced herself against the icy rail and aimed

the big listening cone toward a cluster of small wooden cabins on an island just offshore.

"And you are sure this little guy with the bald head and squeaky voice lives on this island?" Foxtrot asked a small man wrapped in sealskin standing next to her.

"Oh, yes," said the man. "The big island with the totem pole. He is called the chief."

"Perfect," said pirate Echo, connecting the wire from the listening cone to his recorder. "We can listen in. When we hear him, we move in and nab the chief!"

"Sometimes," said the little man in the fur, "the clocks run backward."

Sailor Delta steered the stealth boat around the island. "That sounds like our man."

"No," said Foxtrot. "That sounds like our alien."

Echo listened carefully to the sounds of strange whistling and clicking.

"As soon as we hear him," said Foxtrot, "we make our move!"

AMAZON

åµåΩø˜

Two scientific explorers in pith helmets stood staring at the broad, brownish river flowing in front of them.

"Chief," said a small, barefoot boy wearing Nike shorts and a Dallas Cowboys T-shirt. The boy pointed across the river. Then he pointed to a wooden dugout canoe on the bank.

"Oh, no," said scientist Umber. "Did I tell you that I have a fear of small boats?"

"No, you didn't tell me that," said scientist Hot Magenta. "But you did tell me you have a fear of spiders, a fear of snakes, a fear of tall trees, a fear of diet sodas, and a fear of Reese's peanut butter cups. And what else?"

A brightly colored black and yellow frog hopped down the path behind Umber and Hot Magenta.

"Yikes!" yelled Umber.

"And little brightly colored frogs?" said Hot Magenta.

Umber nodded.

Overhead a band of screeching spider monkeys jumped from tree to tree like something was chasing them.

The boy looked upriver over his shoulder and pointed to the canoe more urgently.

"Now, now. Go chief. Army comes."

A giant horned beetle ran past. A flock of red parrots flew cawing through the underbrush.

Now the boy jumped up and down. He waved both arms. He chomped his teeth.

"Army comes now!" Chomp, chomp, chomp. "You go, go, go!"

"An army?" said Hot Magenta.

The boy waved his arms again, pretending like he was crawling . . . and still biting everything in sight.

"Maybe we can just walk around," said Umber.

"It's the Amazon River, for goodness' sake," said Hot Magenta. "It's thousands of miles long!"

Now the trickle of bugs and birds and monkeys jumping through the jungle had turned into a real rush-hour jam of crawling, hopping, flying creatures.

The boy gave one more look upriver. Then he grabbed Hot Magenta's hand, shook it, and said, "Goods-bye. Have nice day." And he ran off, along with all of the other birds and beasts of the forest, as fast as he could.

"This does not look good," said Hot Magenta.

"Maybe there is a bridge we could walk across?" said Umber.

The screeching and rustling of animals in the jungle grew louder.

Umber walked up the path and looked around the bend in the river for a bridge. He did not see a bridge. But what he did see cured him of his fear of small boats.

"WAAAAAAAAAAAA!!!!!!" screamed Umber, running back to Hot Magenta as fast as he could. Umber jumped in the boat, pulled Hot Magenta in after him, and began paddling furiously. "WAAAAAA! WAAAAAA! ARMY! AAAAAAA! Go, go, go!"

"What?" said Hot Magenta.

"An army," gasped Umber. "Millions!"

And as Umber and Magenta's canoe cleared the jungle bank, an army of millions of ants poured down the path where they had just been. The ants covered the jungle floor and low bushes, swarming, biting, ripping apart any bug, bird, or beast not fast enough to escape their chomping jaws.

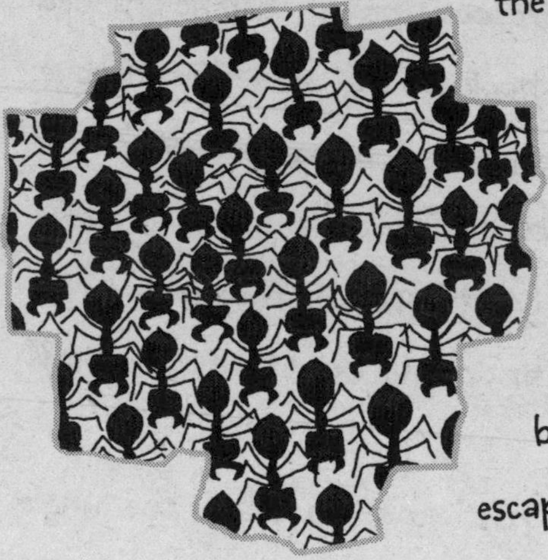

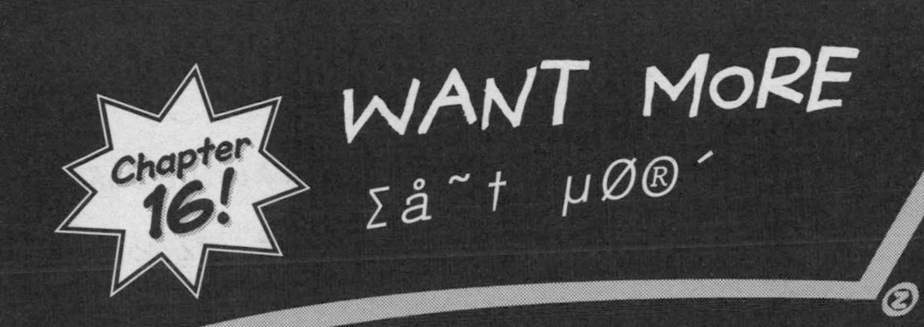

The morning after Graduation Assignment #1, room 501-B was unusually quiet.

Almost every kid in class sat staring off into space.

Every kid except Michael K.

"Did you finish your assignment last night?" Michael K. asked TJ and Venus.

"Yeah," said TJ. "I thought it would be fun. Like eating a big slice of cake. But I don't feel so good. I feel like I ate the whole cake."

"Me too," said Venus. "But I want more."

"***MORE FRUITY FLAVOR,***" said Bob.

"***MORE CLEANING POWER,***" said Jennifer

"Not me," said Michael K. "I don't want to do any more of this."

"BEEEEEEEEEEP," went the class loudspeaker. "Hello. This is your principal. Graduation Assignment Number Two will be completed in class today. Please follow your teacher's directions. That is all."

Almost everyone in 501-B nodded. They wanted more.

Mrs. Halley wrote down Assignment #2 on the blackboard:

Assignment #2

- Continue two hours of TV, one hour of computer, one hour of video games.
- Add one hour of texting friends.
- Add one hour of listening to music.
- Do as many activities as you can at the same time.

"Yes," said Venus.

"We want to," said Bob.

"Why are you guys acting so weird?" said Michael K.

Venus's laptop chimed with an incoming message.

Venus ignored the message alert and started another game of Smashing Fruit!

Venus never ignored an incoming message.

"Venus," said Michael K. "Those are Spaceheadz messages."

"Yeah," said Venus, smashing more fruit.

Michael K. clicked on the incoming message and read it for himself.

"The chief! Team DarkWave X has found him in Alaska! They are making their move to grab him right now!"

Venus's laptop chimed again.

"Wait a minute. Mom, Dad, and my baby sister have found the chief in Florida. They are picking him up right now."

Venus's laptop chimed once more.

"Umber and Hot Magenta in the Amazon. The chief is there.

"Something is very wrong," said Michael K. "The chief can't be in all three places. Which one is it?"

"Ding-ding-ding-ding," rang the tiny fire truck bell.

The line of elephants finished their dance act and filed out of the center ring.

The crowd cheered.

Dad K. peeked out of the fire truck window. He could just see the top of the bald clown's head.

"Perfect," said Dad K. "This is it—we jump out, grab the chief, make it look like part of the act, then throw him in the back of the fire truck and take off before anybody knows what happened."

"Got it," said Mom K., adjusting the single droopy flower on her hat.

"Goo gee gee blaa," warned Baby K.

"Breeee beee," agreed her elephant friend walking by.

But it was too late.

The clown fire truck skidded to a stop. Clown after clown after clown after clown after clown after clown after clown after clown climbed out of the truck.

"Showtime!" shouted Dad K. And he and Mom K. and Baby K. piled on the small, round, bald-headed clown.

"Got you!"

* * *

Foxtrot listened carefully to the clicks and whistles one more time. "That's him, all right."

Foxtrot turned to the sailor and the pirate. "This is it—we bust in, pretend we are pirate/sailor/fisherman, grab the chief, and get back here to the boat before anybody knows what happened."

"Aye, aye," said pirate Echo.

"Anchors aweigh," said sailor Delta.

"Then let's reel him in!" said fisherman Foxtrot.

Delta gunned the engine and ran the stealth boat right up onshore.

The fisherman, sailor, and pirate sprinted up the beach, kicked open the cabin door, and pounced on a small, bald man sitting at his kitchen table.

"Got you!"

* * *

Umber and Hot Magenta crouched behind one gigantic green leaf sprouting from one of the million jungle bushes.

Umber looked through a slit in the leaf at a small, bald man sitting by a fire.

"This is it," whispered Umber. "We rush him, tie him up, and get him out of here before anybody knows what happened."

Hot Magenta pulled her pith helmet down tight on her head. "Okay," she said. "Let's protect and serve and—"

"Always look up," said Umber.

A flock of parrots screeched in the distance.

A line of ants marched down the center of the giant green leaf.

Umber silently flashed his fingers—one . . . two . . . three—and then pointed *Go!*

Umber and Hot Magenta jumped from behind the huge leaf, ran across the soggy jungle floor, and each grabbed an arm of the small, bald guy before he even moved.

"Got you!"

Circle III

The distance from the center of a circle to any point on the circle is called its* radius *(r).

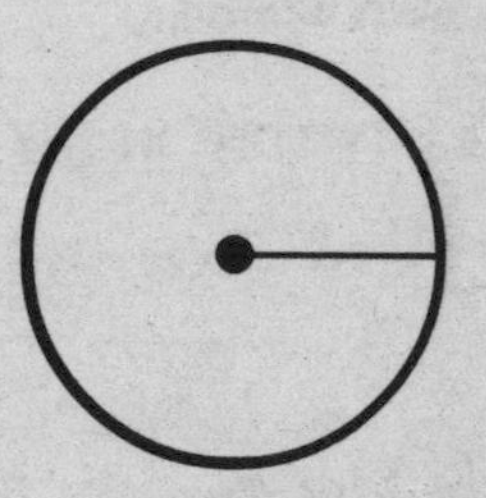

The distance of the radius times itself times π (see "Circle II") equals the* area *(A) of any circle.

$$A = \pi r^2$$

So π times the radius of your circle of friends squared would equal . . . a very powerful area.

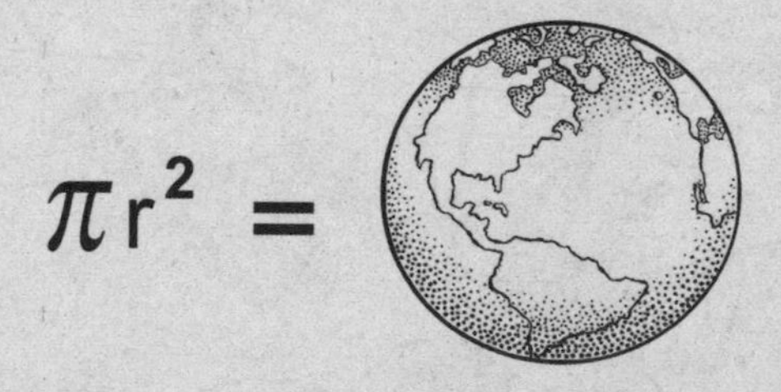

The red-orange rays of the sinking sun glanced off the glass of the TV sets hung over the blackboard in the front of room 501-B.

The kindergartners and the first, second, third, and fourth graders had gone home hours ago.

But the fifth graders of P.S. 858 sat on chairs, desks, and the floor, still working on finishing Assignment #2. Because the fifth graders had special permission from the principal's office to stay in school all day, all night, all week if they wanted.

And they wanted.

TJ and Jennifer ran their players through the twenty-seventh game of Madden NFL.

"Touchdown!" said Jennifer.

"Do you want to play one more?" asked TJ.

"Yes," said Jennifer.

TJ reset for game twenty-eight.

In the Science Corner, Big Joey and his pals Dan and Pete sang the ads for CrispyChicken and double bacon cheeseburgers.

"Do you want to sing one more?" asked Big Joey.

"Yes!" said Pete.

Venus and Major Fluffy watched a video of a dog riding a skateboard, a video of a cat eating peanut butter, a video of a monkey jumping on a bed, a video of a green parrot sleeping on a gray cat.

"Want to watch one more?" said Venus.

"Eee!" said Major Fluffy.

Now Michael K. was really spooked. He liked his TV, video games, and computer as much as anyone. But this was crazy. Even Mrs. Halley had turned into some kind of media-feeding zombie.

"Hey, guys," said Michael K. "The sun is going down. It's late. Let's get out of here and take a break."

Nobody moved.

"Need more," said Bob.

"Want more," said Jennifer.

"More," said Mrs. Halley. She hunched over her video bingo. "One more . . ."

The last of the sun disappeared.

Room 501-B hummed.

Michael K. dropped his head on his desk and drifted off, u-n-c-o-n-s-c-i-o-u-s.

Chapter 19! GOOD NIGHT!

©ØØ∂ ~^©˙†/

Michael K. jolted awake to the sound of blasting and yelling.

PWWWWWOW!

PZZZZINNNGG!

BAZOOOOOAAAANG!

"More!" Mrs. Halley yelled at her computer screen, firing at the swarm of enemies attacking her position.

Mrs. Halley pushed the pile of Hot Tamales boxes and empty Mountain Dew cans off her desk and onto the heap of trash already on the floor.

"More," said Mrs. Halley. "More, more, more!"

No one in room 501-B other than Michael K. seemed to notice they were still in school . . . in the middle of the night.

"**I'M CUCKOO FOR COCOA PUFFS,**" said TJ, finishing off a box of Count Chocula and shooting down two Space Invaders.

"**IT'S THE REAL THING,**" said Bob, chomping a fistful of Cap'n Crunch's Crunch Berries and choosing the hairstyle for his pony in My Little Pony: Pinkie Pie's Party Parade.

"**FINGER LICKIN' GOOD,**" said Jennifer, eating the last of her twelve-pack of Crayola colored pencils and jumping her WWF SmackDown! Just Bring It video game wrestler off the top of a ladder.

Big Joey and his pals sat on the floor in the corner, surrounded by half-empty bags of Flamin' Hot Cheetos, Lay's Barbecue chips, Sea Salt and Vinegar, Sour Cream and Onion, Honey Dijon, Lime and Chili, Pepper Bacon, Jalapeño, Four Cheese, Dill Pickle, New York Cheddar, Toasted, Baked,

Chile Picante, Nacho, and Zesty Ranch Chips, and Original, Cheddar Cheese, and Honey Mustard Pringles. . . .

They seemed to be having a discussion.

"NOBODY CAN EAT JUST ONE."

"HAVE IT YOUR WAY."

"THE BEST PART OF WAKING UP . . . IS FOLGERS IN YOUR CUP."

Major Fluffy dug tunnels in a nest of wrappers from Almond Joy, Twix, Goo Goo Clusters, Milky Way, Snickers, Baby Ruth, Nestlé Crunch, Reese's Pieces, Peanut, Pretzel, and plain M&M'S, Mr. Goodbar, Kit Kat, Butterfinger, York Peppermint Pattie, Mallo Cup, Tootsie Roll, Mounds, Heath bar, 5th Avenue, Bit-O-Honey, Oh Henry!, PayDay, 100 Grand, 3 Musketeers, and NutRageous candy bars.

"More Red Hots! More Hot Tamales!" shouted Mrs. Halley.

"This is just weird," said Michael K., mostly to himself because no one was listening.

"BEEEEEEEEEEEEP," went the speaker over the classroom door. "Attention. Attention. Very good work on your graduation assignments. Michael K., please report to the principal's office."

"Whaaa?" said Michael K.

"Immediately," said the buzzing speaker.

"Move, soldier!" barked Mrs. Halley, mowing down a row of attackers. "And get me some more Hot Tamales and Red Hots while you are down there!"

"Yes, Mrs. Halley," Michael K. shouted back.

Michael K. jumped up from his seat and ran down to the office without thinking. The squeak of his sneakers on the shiny floors echoed in the empty hallways.

Michael K. ran down the stairs. He ran to the main office. He looked at the school clock. He stopped. Then he started thinking.

What was he doing in school at three in the morning?

Why was room 501-B so crazy about wanting to do these weird graduation assignments?

Something was not right.

Michael K. looked out the front school doors to the deserted street outside.

Should he just walk out? Go get help?

Or should he report to the principal's office? In the middle of the night?

The big black hand of the school clock ticked over to 3:01.

Michael K. decided this was just too strange. He turned and headed for the front doors. And that's when he heard a familiar humming noise coming from behind the door with the sign

Michael K. forgot about going to get help.

Michael K. forgot about Mrs. Halley's Hot Tamales and Red Hots.

Michael K decided he was going to get some answers for himself.

Michael K. grabbed the doorknob on the principal's office door. He turned the knob and swung open the door.

Altruism I

Altruism is behaving in a way that helps others but puts an individual's welfare at risk.

Vervet monkeys give an alarm call when they see a predator like a tiger.

This helps the other monkeys, who get the warning . . . but it puts the noisy alarm monkey in more danger.

Vampire bats puke up blood they have eaten to feed other bats in their group who haven't eaten. This helps the bats that couldn't find food, but means the puking bat gets less food.

Giving the alarm call that your mom is coming when you and your brothers are grabbing cookies from the cookie jar is a good example of altruism.

Puking up your Brussels sprouts so your sister can eat them is not.

The small, bald-headed clown rolled over in the circus sawdust.

"What are you clowns doing? You are ruining the show!"

Dad K. had a sudden sinking feeling.

"Uh-oh. This is not the chief."

* * *

The small, bald-headed man at the kitchen table laughed.

"Why are you dressed for Halloween?"

Fisherman Foxtrot had a sudden sinking feeling.

"Uh-oh. This is not the chief."

* * *

The small, bald-headed man stood next to the fire.

"Qual é o seu problema?"

Umber had a sudden sinking feeling.

"Uh-oh. This is definitely not the chief."

Chapter 21! TROUBLE IN THE PRINCIPAL'S OFFICE

The small, bald-headed man sitting at the principal's desk spread open his arms.

"Michael K.! We meet at last."

Michael K. had a sudden sinking feeling.

"Uh-oh. Chief?"

"The one and only," said the chief.

"But . . . but . . . but what are you doing here? You are supposed to be in Alaska! Or Florida! Or the Amazon! And what did you do with our new principal?"

The chief chewed on the end of a red pencil. "Oh, I am your new principal."

"Oh, no," said Michael K.

"Oh, yes," said the chief. "And I'm so glad to see you. Because you have something I need."

"I don't have anything you need," said Michael K. "*You* have our Spaceheadz Brainwave. You stole it. And we want it back."

"Of course you do," said the chief, eating the rest of the red pencil. "That's why I've been softening you up . . . I mean, that's why I invited you down to my office."

Michael K. looked around the principal's office. It didn't look like a principal's office anymore. It looked more like the laboratory of a mad scientist.

Half of it was filled with a thing that looked like a giant ray gun, labeled

RED-HOT RAY

A sparking blue snow globe sat on the principal's desk.

And where the principal's fish tank used to be, a single lunchroom chair sat on top of a large, humming black egg-shaped thing.

"Hey, that's the noise I recognized. That's our IWANT Pulsar!"

The chief walked around the desk to get closer to Michael K. "Yes, yes, yes. And you can have that back too." The chief put a goofy aluminum foil hat on his head and turned a dial on the IWANT Pulsar. The black egg hummed louder. "Right after you sit down in the chair and we take care of the last bit of Brainwave business."

Michael K. looked at the chair on top of the IWANT Pulsar. "I don't think I want to," said Michael K.

The chief turned the dial on the IWANT Pulsar up to eleven.

"Now you want to."

Michael K. looked around. "No, I don't," said Michael K.

The chief turned the dial to twelve. The black egg hummed louder and wobbled.

"Now you definitely want to."

"No, I definitely don't."

The chief's face flushed a bit red. He squeezed the aluminum foil hat on his head tight with both hands. Then he cranked the IWANT Pulsar up to twenty.

The black egg whined like a jet engine.

"Now you want to. Sit down and GIVE ME YOUR BRAIN WAVE!"

"Hmmmm," said Michael K. "Nope. Still don't want to."

The chief freaked out. He pounded the desk with both fists. He smacked his forehead with both hands.

"This is terrible!" said the chief. "Your puny brain resists the WantWaves. And that is also why your one brain wave didn't load. You don't believe the wanting/needing/having will make you faster/stronger/better."

The school clock on the wall behind him stopped, then spun backward fast, faster and faster until the hands flew right off the clock and stuck into the wall like two daggers.

"Well, of course," said Michael K. "That's just advertising. I've known that since I was a kid. Just because you eat SuperCrunchies doesn't mean you can really do anything."

"Ohhhhhhhhhh," said the chief, suddenly realizing he could not get Michael K.'s brain wave unless Michael K. wanted to give it up.

"Ahhhhhhh," said Michael K., suddenly realizing the chief could not do anything without his plus one brain wave.

"Okay," said the chief. "We could have done this the easy way. But now we are going to do it the hard way."

The chief picked up what looked like an ordinary stapler and aimed it directly between Michael K.'s eyes.

Michael K. had a bad feeling that this was not an ordinary stapler. And he was right.

The chief fired his stapler.

The last thing Michael K. saw before he went u-n-c-o-n-s-c-i-o-u-s was a blue-white bolt of pure energy coming right at him.

Chapter 22! TROUBLE IN THE SUNSHINE STATE

Mom K. pushed a pile of elephant plop onto Dad K.'s shovel. Dad K. dropped the stinky mess into the trash can Baby K. wheeled over.

Dad K. muttered, "What a pile of—"

"Shoot!" interrupted Mom K., tugging at the elephant chain attached to her ankle. "We have to get these off and track down the real chief."

Dad K. tugged at his own ankle chain and scooped another pile into the trash. "Try telling that to the head clown again. He said we will have to work a whole week to earn him back the money he lost on the show we ruined."

"Goo glah goo goo," suggested Baby K., slipping out of her chain.

"Breeee beeee beee," agreed a big bull elephant. And then he dropped another hot, wet, steaming pile of—

"Shoot!" said Mom K.

"We have to get out of here," said Dad K.

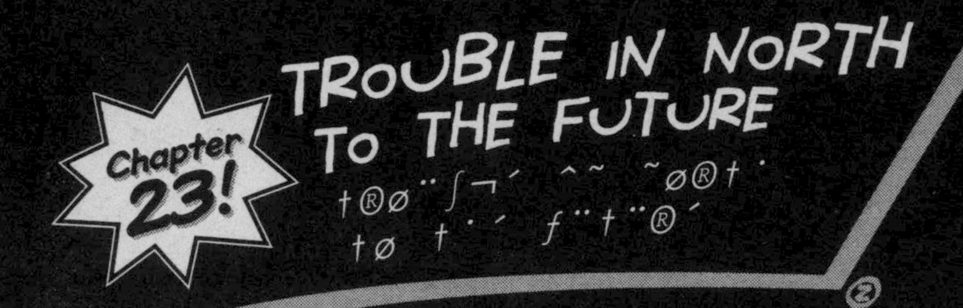

Chapter 23! TROUBLE IN NORTH TO THE FUTURE

†®ø¨∫¬´ ^~ ˜ø®†˙
†ø †˙´ ƒ¨†¨®´

A
gain," said the small, bald man at the kitchen table.

"Do we have to?" said pirate Echo, tied to one of the kitchen chairs, with some very fancy fishing knots in the thick white rope.

"Yes," said the man. "I don't often get a crew to help me sing my old sea chanteys. So nice of you to drop in."

And then the crusty old man started to sing, with fisherman Foxtrot, sailor Delta, and pirate Echo answering.

"As I was a-walking down Paradise Street."

"Way, hey, blow the man down."

"A pretty young damsel I happened to meet."

"Give me some time to blow the man down."

"Oh, man," said fisherman Foxtrot. "There must be a hundred verses to this song."

"Two hundred," groaned sailor Delta.

"We have got to get out of here and get back on the trail of the real chief," said pirate Echo.

"So I tailed her my flipper and took her in tow."

"Way, hey, blow the man down."

"And yardarm to yardarm away we did go."

"Give me some time to blow the man down."

"We really have to get out of here," said Agent Foxtrot.

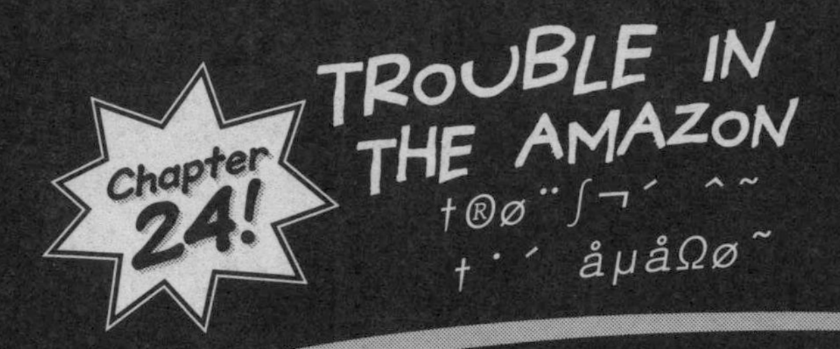

Chapter 24! TROUBLE IN THE AMAZON

Umber and Hot Magenta stood back-to-back, tied to a tree in the middle of the Amazon jungle.

Red and green parrots screeched in the branches overhead.

It started to rain.

Umber wiggled one hand back and forth against the wet rope.

"Ouch," said Hot Magenta.

"Sorry," said Umber. "But I think I've almost got it." Umber wiggled. Umber waggled. Umber twisted one hand free.

"Bzzzzrt," buzzed Umber's pocket. "Bzzzzrt."

Umber used his free hand to pull out his Picklephone®.

"Oh, no," said Umber. "Huge AEW spike at D-7. That's back at P.S. 858. Maybe it's the chief."

"Not possible," said Hot Magenta. "Our data says the chief is here."

"But that was not the chief who tied us up." Umber untied his other hand, then untied Hot Magenta. He looked at the AEW warning on his Picklephone® again. "I've got a bad feeling about this."

"Probably just a glitch," answered Hot Magenta, brushing dirt off her khaki pants. "We cleared that whole area D-7."

The rain splattered on the leaves above.

Umber thought.

Umber came up with a plan.

"We've been tricked," said Umber. "Something big is happening back at P.S. 858. And we really, really have to get out of here."

Altruism II

Some animals take advantage of other animals' altruistic behavior for their own gain.

The European common cuckoo lays its eggs in other birds' nests.

The other birds raise the baby cuckoo when it hatches, even though this doesn't help their bird family.

Cuckoo bees and cuckoo wasps likewise lay their eggs in the nests of other bees and wasps . . . and let them do all of the bee and wasp nesting and young-raising work.

So it would probably be a good idea to be very suspicious of anyone named Cuckoo.

Back in room 501-B no one was missing Michael K. because everyone was completely blasted by the cranked-up WantWaves.

And everyone was surrounded by piles of products that had been bought and instantly delivered all day and all night by AAA Speedy Express vans.

Jennifer arranged her infomercial collection like it was a pile of treasure. She spoke to each item as she touched it:

"Belly Burner! **THE AMAZING WEIGHT-LOSS BELT.**

"Power Trainer Pro! **FITS MOST DOORWAYS IN SECONDS.**

"AB Rocket! **BLAST YOUR ABS LIKE NEVER BEFORE.**

"Shake Weight! **THIS IS NOT A WORKOUT, IT'S A REVOLUTION.**

"Shipping and handling extra."

Bob rolled around in his pile and babbled:

"Pajama Jeans! **THE LOOK OF JEANS WITH THE COMFORT OF PAJAMAS.**

"Slanket! **THE ORIGINAL BLANKET WITH SLEEVES.**

"Snuggie! **AFFORDABLE FOR ANY BUDGET.**

"BeDazzler! **MAKE DULL INTO DAZZLING.**

"Act now. Special offer. Three easy payments."

TJ stacked a pyramid of Coke, Pepsi, Diet Coke, Mountain Dew, Diet Pepsi, Dr Pepper, Sprite, Fanta, Diet Mountain Dew, Cherry Coke, Dad's root beer, Canada Dry ginger ale, Cherry Coke Zero, Fresca, Jolt cola, Coke Zero, Mello Yello, RC cola, Slice, Sierra Mist, caffeine-free Coke, Shasta cola, Squirt, and 7UP cans.

TJ spoke to his pyramid. "**THE PAUSE THAT REFRESHES. THE REAL THING. JUST FOR THE TASTE OF IT. MAXIMUM TASTE, ZERO CALORIES. DO THE DEW. IT'S THAT REFRESHING. OBEY YOUR THIRST. BE YOU.**"

Venus chanted what sounded like a poem in an invented language:

"Lunesta, Crestor, Flomax, Lipitor.

Nasonex, Allegra, Visine . . .

LEAVE THE REST TO US.

NOW YOU'RE GETTING IT.

RELIEVES CONGESTION FOR HOURS.

AND GETS THE RED OUT."

Major Fluffy burrowed frantic tunnels in his candy wrapper mountain.

"EEEEK EEE EEEE!

"WEEEK EEE EEE EEE.

"SQUEEE EEEK WEEEEK."

Major Fluffy laughed. He jumped into his spinning hamster wheel. He ran like a maniac, then spun around inside the wheel once, twice, three times . . . and flew out, landing in his shredded candy wrappers with a **BOOM!**

"Turbo hamster!" cheered TJ.

Major Fluffy jumped in the wheel, spun around, and flipped out again.

And again.

And again.

And again.

PWWWWWOW!

PZZZZINNNGG!

BAZOOOOOAAAANG!

Mrs. Halley mowed down all attackers.

"More ammo!" shouted Mrs. Halley. "Where are my Hot Tamales and Red Hots?! Where is Michael K.?!"

Michael K. was sitting in the principal's office, tied to a lunchroom chair with a plastic rainbow-colored gym class jump rope.

Michael K. struggled to escape.

"You can't make me give you my brain wave," said Michael K.

"Oh, no?" said the chief. "We'll see about that."

"What are you going to do? Drill into my skull? Electro-zap my nerve cells? Suck my brains out of my ears?"

"Eeeeewww," said the chief. "That is disgusting."

The chief munched on a fresh red pencil like it was a Twizzler. "No, I have something much more effective."

"I'll never give it up," said Michael K. "Kids joined Spaceheadz to save the world. You are a bad guy. And I am not going to give you the power to destroy everything."

The chief dug into his crate. He pulled out a brightly colored jumble of plush fish and starfish and crabs, all hanging from the arms of a purple plastic octopus. He hung the baby mobile in front of Michael K.

"Are you kidding me?" said Michael K.

The chief turned on the motorized mobile. The creepy smiling fish and starfish and crabs started slowly spinning around. A mindless, happy song started playing.

"Oh, I am not kidding you," said the chief. The chief picked up the sparking blue snow globe off his principal's desk. "Your brain may be ad resistant and IWANT resistant. But a couple hours of this . . . and you will be begging me to take your brain wave.

The Ocean Wonders animals spun in their slow circle.

The Ocean Wonders song started over again.

This was both creepy and annoying.

Michael K. started to feel just a little bit worried.

Michael K. strained against the jump rope. "My team will save me."

The chief laughed. "Your team is a mess! The fifth graders are all want-heads. Your SPHDZ are even more want-crazy and useless. And the rest of your team is scattered around the globe. No one is coming to save you."

The purple octopus twirled.

The Ocean Wonders song started again.

Michael K. tried to tip his little chair over. But he couldn't even do that. He hoped the chief was wrong. But he had a terrible feeling he was right.

The purple octopus twirled.

The Ocean Wonders song started again.

Michael K. felt himself going just a little crazy.

He hoped the chief wasn't right about his team.

He hoped someone was on the way to save him.

MEANWHILE IN FLORIDA, ALASKA, AND THE AMAZON

µ´å˜∑˙ˆ¬´ ˆ˜ ƒ¬ø®ˆ∂å,
å¬åß˚å, å˜∂ †˙´ åµåΩø˜

Mom K. sat down next to the full, stinky can of elephant plop.

"This is terrible. We are trapped."

* * *

DarkWave X agent Delta tried to plug his ears so he wouldn't hear the old man singing anymore.

"This is horrible," said DarkWave X agent Foxtrot. "We are stuck."

* * *

Hot Magenta poked at the small fire outside a hut in the jungle.

She looked up at the stars, which reminded her of her AAA pledge, which reminded her of Agent Umber.

She was pretty sure the chief was here in the Amazon and that she would catch him.

And she was pretty sure Umber's AEW spike at P.S. 858 was a mistake.

But if it wasn't, she sure hoped Umber got there in time.

MEANWHILE IN ROOM 501–B

µ´å˜∑˙ˆ¬´ ˆ˜
®øøµ ∞º¡-∫

PWWWWWOW!

PZZZZINNNGG!

BAZOOOOOAAAANG!

Mrs. Halley fired her weapons and racked up her 375th mission.

"IT SLICES AND DICES," Bob explained to Jennifer.

"RED BULL GIVES YOU WINGS," said TJ.

"But Aleve is **ALL DAY STRONG, ALL DAY LONG,"** answered Venus.

Major Fluffy ate another Almond Joy.

He jumped into his wheel, ran like mad, spun around, and flipped out again.

And again.

And again.

No one in room 501-B was going anywhere or saving anyone anytime soon.

Chapter 29! THE PURPLE OCTOPUS

The purple octopus spun slowly overhead for hours.

Michael K. wobbled. His head was full of weird sea creatures and that nonstop xylophone tune.

"Now?" said the chief.

Michael K. took a deep breath. He shook his head.

"Never."

"Arrrrrrrr!" yelled the chief.

"Beep," beeped the coffeemaker on the chief's desk. And then it started talking. "Brew finished. Chief, report!"

The chief jumped like he had been shocked. "General Accounting!" the chief squeaked in a very high voice. "It is so good to hear from you."

"What is report?" hissed the coffeemaker. "Gonf must be bllrrped NOW!"

"Oh, yes!" said the chief. "I've got everything under control." The chief looked frantically around his office. "Just about ready . . ."

"No more time, Chief," said the coffeemaker. "You are—"

"All set!" said the chief. "We are all set for graduation! It's a very big ceremony here on Earth. Perfect for bllrrping Gonf!"

"PSSSSSSS," said the coffeemaker.

The chief grabbed the microphone for the school PA system. "Here, listen! I was just going to make the announcement to all of the Earth persons." The chief pressed the speak button on the microphone. "Attention, all classes. Attention. This is your principal. I have decided that school is over. Graduation is tomorrow at noon. And I have a very big surprise for everyone."

Michael K. heard the sound of surprised cheers from the classrooms.

"Hmmmmmm," said the coffeemaker. "Earth tomorrow at noon. That is the End. Beep!" The coffeemaker powered off.

The chief plopped down in his chair. He looked at Michael K.

"Now it's time to get serious."

* * *

Outside the principal's office the kids and teachers of P.S. 858 chattered and hummed with excitement. Graduation tomorrow. Summer vacation was coming early.

In room 501-B, Mrs. Halley and her fifth graders were a mess.

Everyone had crashed. And crashed hard. Kids were sprawled on tables, curled in the Science Corner, passed out under the math bins, snoring facedown on their laptop keyboards.

Mrs. Halley sat perfectly upright in her chair, but her eyes were closed, and she was furiously dreaming of winning Math Blaster and mowing down enemy attackers.

* * *

Inside the principal's office was an even bigger mess.

The chief unleashed every AAA and evil intergalactic trick he knew to break Michael K.

The chief tried sad-eyed puppies, elevator music, flashing neon lights.

Michael K. still said no.

Morning turned into afternoon.

All of the kids and teachers, except room 501-B, went home to get ready for Graduation tomorrow.

The chief tried snakes and spiders, terrible smells, promises of candy.

Michael K. still said no.

Afternoon turned into evening.

Room 501-B woke up and started gaming, watching, and wanting again.

The chief tried foot tickling, scary stories, offers of fame and money.

Michael K. still said no.

Evening turned into night.

Except for classroom 501-B and the principal's office, P.S. 858 was dark and quiet.

"This is getting ridiculous," said Michael K.

"Yes, it is," said the chief. "It's time you gave me that brain wave. Because now I'll use the last resort."

The chief held up a small black plastic rectangle with colored buttons.

"Ooooooh," said Michael K. "A TV remote. Very scary."

The chief smiled a mean smile. "Oh, but this is not any remote. This is not a remote that changes channels. This remote changes Energy Waves."

Michael K. remembered seeing the remote somewhere before.

"You saw this remote on the first day of school," said the chief, like he was reading Michael K.'s thoughts. "Your SPHDZ friends stupidly used it to change forms. It is also how we SPHDZ travel. By changing energy channels."

"So what?" said Michael K. "So you are going to change me into a wrestler or a unicorn?"

"Oh, no," said the chief. "I am going to change you into a worm. A small, disgusting, slimy worm." The chief aimed the remote at Michael K. "So this is it. Your last chance. I won't get your brain wave. But you will be nothing but a worm. Give me your brain wave or—"

A metallic crash sounded just outside the principal's office.

The chief froze. He tiptoed quietly over to the door. He grabbed the doorknob and whipped the door open.

He could not believe what he saw.

"What?!" said the chief. "You?!"

Brain I

Early scientists explained how the brain works by using hydraulic models. Ideas and emotions and behaviors were thought to be caused by pressures and imbalances of humors that worked like liquids.

A good name for this model would be the plumbing model.

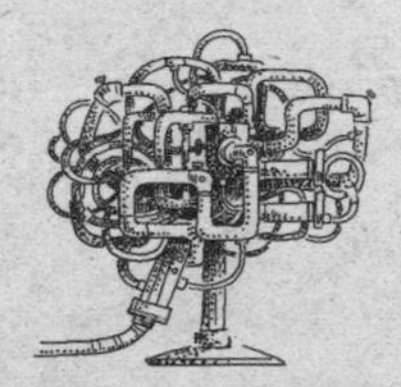

Later scientists explained how the brain works by using mechanical and clockwork models.

Let's call this the machine model.

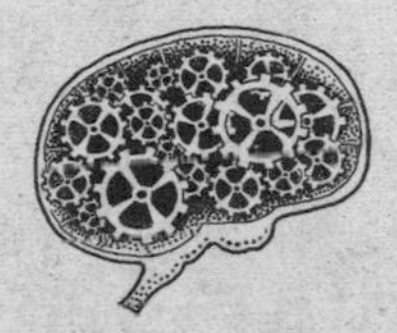

Recent scientists explain how the brain works using electronic and computer models.

You know what to call this model.

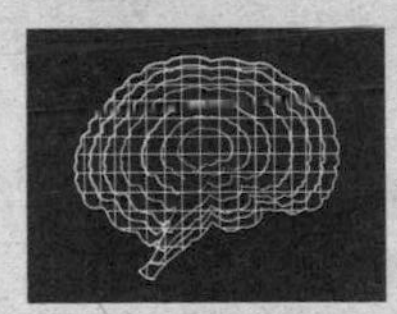

And now scientists are learning that the brain grows and changes.

What do you think we will think of the brain next?

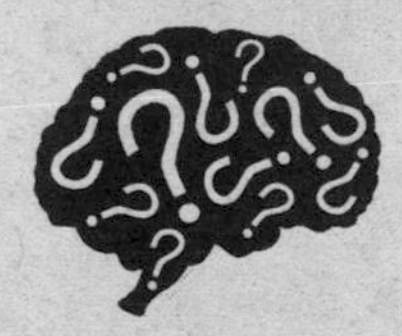

JUST A FEW MINUTES EARLIER

∆¨ßt å f´∑
µ^~¨t´ß ´å®¬^´®

Major Fluffy jumped into his hamster wheel.

Again.

Major Fluffy started racing.

Again.

Major Fluffy spun around and around and flipped out of the wheel.

Again.

But this time Major Fluffy fell into a foil wedge of a Hershey's Kiss wrapper, which wrapped his head like a perfect hat.

The buzzing and humming and wanting inside Fluffy's head suddenly stopped.

Major Fluffy sat up and looked around room 501-B. He wondered what the heck everyone was doing still playing away in the middle of the night.

"**CHANGE YOUR LIFE IN THIRTY DAYS!**" said Jennifer.

"**MICROFIBER COMFORT!**" cheered Bob.

"**THE RELIEF GOES ON!**" said Venus.

Major Fluffy stood on top of his cage to tell everyone that this was crazy, they were all being controlled by WantWaves, that Michael K. was in trouble in the principal's office, and that they all needed to go save him. Right now.

Major Fluffy banged his water bowl on his wheel.

Everyone in room 501-B paused and looked up.

Major Fluffy explained, "Eeeee eeek weeek eeek! Weee eeek eee eee, eek ee eeeek, week weee wee eee eee eeek, eeek eeek eeek eeek, eee weee eeeek, eek eeeek eee eeek weeek weeek wee we we we, wee eee eek. Eeeek eee."

"Yes," answered Bob. "And it removes lint from hard-to-reach places."

Fluffy tried again.

"Bark bark woof! Woof!"

"ZERO CALORIES. MAXIMUM PEPSI TASTE," said TJ.

"Goo goo gah?"

Mrs. Halley yelled, **"REMEMBER REACH! FINISH THE FIGHT!"**

Nobody was getting it.

Major Fluffy desperately tried a few of his other languages.

"Meow cheep honk tweet oink snort ribbit bweeee!"

Venus looked up. You could almost see her thinking. And then she said: "Side effects may include dizziness, diarrhea, vomiting, ringing in the ears, a bad taste in your mouth, and limited brain function for life."

Major Fluffy collapsed back into his pile of candy wrappers.

This was not good.

Everyone was too media zonked out to hear anything.

Someone had to save Michael K. And that someone was a Spaceheadz in the form of a fifth-grade class hamster.

Major Fluffy took one more bite of a Nestlé Crunch bar, slid down the leg of the science table, and sneaked out of room 501-B and down the night-quiet hallways of P.S. 858.

Major Fluffy didn't know what he was going to do. But he knew he had to do something to save Michael K. . . . and the world.

A ragged taco wearing Elmo slippers flattened himself against the outside brick wall of P.S. 858.

It was the middle of the night, but light blazed from two rooms.

The taco looked at a diagram of the school floor plan on his Picklephone® and said, "The principal's office . . . and room 501-B. I was right! I knew something was wrong here."

The taco slippered quietly up the stairs and through the unlocked main door.

Something was definitely wrong.

Though the taco disguise was pretty darn good.

Bam! "Oooof!" The taco bumped his head on the cardboard HAPPY GRADUATION sign.

The taco dived flat on the floor and listened for an alarm.

Nothing.

No, wait.

The sound of a voice. Two voices. One squeaky. One not so squeaky. Coming from the main office. The principal's office.

The taco crawled along the floor. He wormed into the office, behind the desk. The voices were arguing.

The taco stood up very slowly, very quietly. The most valuable weapon in a situation like this would be the element of surprise.

The taco edged slowly toward the door marked

The taco reached for the doorknob and . . . *CRASH!* knocked a pencil-filled Folgers coffee can to the floor.

Taco Umber froze.

The principal's door whipped open.

Umber could not believe what he saw.

"What?!" said the chief. "You?!"

Taco Umber tried a quick AAA karate chop attack but forgot that his arms were stuck inside his taco. Umber fell forward, knocking the chief back into the room.

"Aieeeeee!" yelled the chief, dropping the Spaceheadz remote.

He waved his short little arms but couldn't balance himself. He couldn't stop from falling backward against the giant metal ray gun.

The chief hit his head with a *BOING* and was knocked out cold.

"Agent Umber!" said Michael K. "You did it!"

"I did?" said Umber, still not sure exactly what he had done.

"Quick, untie me. We have got to get the rest of our Spaceheadz team and get out of here!"

Taco Umber fumbled with the knots in the jump rope.

The chief moaned.

"Faster," said Michael K.

"The knots are too tight!" said the taco.

The chief rolled over onto his hands and knees.

"He's waking up!" said Michael K., because that's all he could do.

Taco Umber decided to forget the knots. He scooped up Michael K., chair and all, and ran out of the office, bouncing off the doorway, the file cabinets, and the desks on the way out.

"Stop!" yelled the chief, staggering to his feet. "Give me that Michael K. brain wave!"

The chief grabbed his stapler and fired a blast that smoked Umber's lettuce.

Umber ran down the hall, ducking and dodging and carrying Michael K. at the same time.

"Stop!" yelled the chief.

Taco Umber made it to the top of the stairs. "We'll have to come back for everybody else."

Umber hopped down the stairs as fast as he could.

"Go, Umber, go!" said Michael K.

The chief's stapler blasts bounced off the tile walls and floors.

Umber bent over to shoulder open the door.

The chief lined up his stapler for one perfect shot and fired.

BZZZZZZZTTTT!

The laser blast hit Umber square in his taco butt.

The blast knocked Umber down the stairs. But he landed miraculously on his Elmo-slippered feet and ran off safely into the night with Michael K., still tied to the lunchroom chair.

The chief, too late, burst out of the front doors.

"You think you got away!" the chief yelled at the dark street. "But I've still got your friends!"

Umber stopped running for a second and turned around.

"Give me your brain wave or I will change every one of your friends' channels tomorrow at graduation!"

The chief turned back and walked into school, fuming. He was mad. So mad that he never even saw a small hamster in a foil candy wrapper hat slip outside just before the school doors closed.

Back at Spaceheadz HQ, Umber used Bob's Dora safety scissors to snip off the last of the jump rope holding Michael K.

"Agent Umber. You saved my life."

Michael K. fell out of the chair, rubbing his sore wrists. He was so thrilled to be out of the principal's office, and so glad to see Umber. He told Umber everything in one long sentence.

"You are not going to believe it, but the chief got rid of the rest of our team by having them chase fake chiefs all over the world so he could sneak into school and disguise himself as principal and turn everyone into want-zombies by using the IWANT Pulsar so he could get my one brain wave, which did not load into the Brainwave globe because I can resist it, which is why he can't fire the Red-Hot Ray to bllrrp Gonf and take over the universe!"

"Wow," said Umber, peeling off his taco.

"You can say that again," said Michael K.

"Wow," said Umber.

"No, I didn't mean . . . oh, never mind." Michael K. paced back and forth. "We have to get everyone back here now."

"I'll send out the word on my Picklephone®," said Umber.

Umber pulled his Picklephone® out of the laser-scorched butt pocket of his taco disguise. The Picklephone® was a laser-blasted blob of melted plastic and metal.

"Oh, no," said Michael K.

Umber cradled his Picklephone® sadly. "Poor little guy got fried, but he saved my butt."

"Now we are fried. We can't contact anyone. Venus has all the secret contacts on her laptop."

The TVs that were always on at Spaceheadz HQ flickered five different late-night talk shows.

"There must be something we can do with all of our Spaceheadz."

Michael K. used the Spaceheadz computer to log on to spaceheadz.com. He checked the latest counter number.

"Look at all of these Spaceheadz who are still signing up to help us! Nobody even knows this is a fake counter to hide the terrible news that the chief stole the Brainwave. . . . There must be something we can do. Some way we can use our Spaceheadz to fight the chief. We can't let everyone down."

"Eeek weee ee eeek."

Michael K. looked up from spaceheadz.com. "I didn't know you spoke Hamster, Agent Umber."

"I didn't say anything," said Umber.

"Weee eeee eee," came the voice again.

"It's coming from outside the door," whispered Umber. "It sounds like Major Fluffy."

"But he's still trapped in school," whispered Michael K. "It must be a trick. You open the door. I will whack whoever it is."

Umber nodded.

Michael K. tiptoed over to the door, picked up Jennifer's New York Rangers hockey stick, and raised it over his head.

Umber flung open the door.

"EEEEEEEEeeeee!" squeaked a hamster wearing a tinfoil cap on his head.

Michael K. couldn't stop himself. He swung the hockey stick and smashed it down with all his strength.

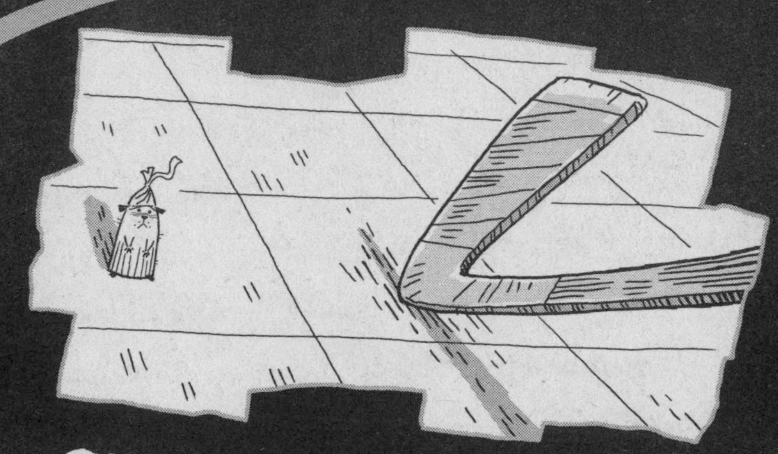

CRAAACK! went the hockey stick.

"EEEEK!" went Major Fluffy.

But luckily for Major Fluffy and the future of the universe, Michael K. was a terrible hockey player.

He missed Fluffy by a mile.

"Sorry, Major Fluffy," said Michael K. "We thought you might be someone else."

"Squee eee? Squee eeek weee eeek?" asked Major Fluffy. Then he quickly ran inside HQ.

Umber shut and locked the Spaceheadz HQ door behind him.

"Thank goodness you are here, Major Fluffy," said Umber. "We are in a total pickle."

"Weee ee ee," said Major Fluffy. "Eeeeek eeek eek eee?"

Major Fluffy looked at Umber and Michael K., waiting for an answer to his question.

Michael K. and Umber looked at each other. Neither understood a word of what Major Fluffy had just said.

Michael K. sat down at Jennifer's computer again. He clicked on Major Fluffy's "eeek!" section.

Then he clicked on

On the right side of that page, Michael K. clicked on

A translation box appeared.

"Okay," said Michael K. "What did you say?"

Major Fluffy repeated, "Weee ee ee. Eeeeek eeek eek eee?"

Michael K. typed, translated, then read what Major Fluffy had said: "'The chief must be stopped. What are we going to do?'"

Michael K. held his head in his hands. He felt dizzy, beat up, and completely empty. "I just don't know. If I don't agree to give the chief my brain wave, he is going to really mess up Bob and Jennifer and TJ and Venus."

Agent Umber peeled off his taco. "But if you do give it to him, he is going to use it to bllrrp Gonf, then turn off Earth. And that will mess up everyone."

Michael K. groaned. Why did this all have to happen to him? "My brain wave will give the chief the power of our whole network. I wish we had an even bigger network to smash him. We need a giant army."

"Yeah," said Umber, taking off his Elmo slippers. "Like the whole army of ants I saw in the Amazon. There were millions."

Fluffy sat up on his hind legs. "EEEE! Eeee eeeek eeek!"

Michael K. leaned back in his chair and stared at the ceiling. "Yeah. Like a huge herd of animals . . ."

"EEEE! Eeek eek eeek!" said Fluffy, tugging at Michael K.'s pants.

"Or a school of fish . . . ," added Umber.

"EEEEK!" squeaked Fluffy as loud as he could.

"Or all of those flocks and herds and colonies of insects we read about in our science book all year," said Michael K.

Major Fluffy ran in a circle. Major Fluffy jumped up and down. Neither Umber nor Michael K. paid any attention to him. Major Fluffy decided it was time for drastic action. Major Fluffy pulled down the top of Michael K.'s sock. He opened his mouth as wide as he could . . .

and bit down on Michael K.'s ankle with his needle-sharp teeth.

"YOOOOOOOWWWWWWWW!" yelled Michael K. He shook Major Fluffy off his ankle. "What did you do that for?"

"Eeeee EEEE!" explained Major Fluffy. "Eeeee eeee eeek eeee!"

Major Fluffy pointed to the translator.

"Oh, sorry," said Michael K.

"EEEK eeee," said Major Fluffy very slowly and carefully so Michael K. could type it in. "Eeek weee eee weee."

Umber read the translation over Michael K.'s shoulder. "'That is it. You are exactly right.'"

"Exactly right about what?" said Michael K.

"Weeeek eeek eek eek. Eeeek eee eee eeeek."

"'There are networks bigger than Spaceheadz already on Earth.'"

"Eeeek weee eee eee ekekeke."

"'They are networks of your Earth animals: elephants, whales, and ants.'"

"Eeeek weeee weeee eee ee eee ee."

"'Just as you have in your science book.'"

Michael K. fell back in his chair. "No."

"Yeek!"

"Bigger?"

"Yeek!"

"And we could use their power to cancel out the chief's Red-Hot Ray power?"

"Yeeek yeek!"

"Wow," said Umber. "The answer was right in front of us the whole time!"

"But how do we contact the ant, elephant, and whale networks?" asked Michael K. "How do we get them to help us in time to stop the chief at Graduation tomorrow?"

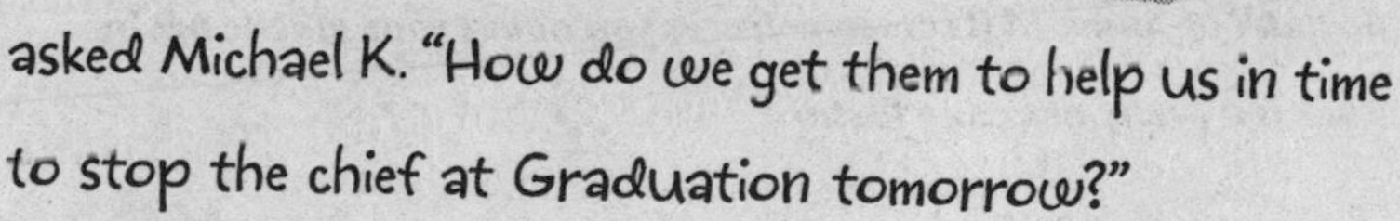

Major Fluffy smiled.

"Breeeee bee beee! Beooooowuuuuuoooooooooo! Tap tap taptaptap!" said Major Fluffy, speaking Elephant, Whale, and Ant all together.

Brain II

Your brain never stops changing.

Using your brain cells physically changes the connections between brain cells.

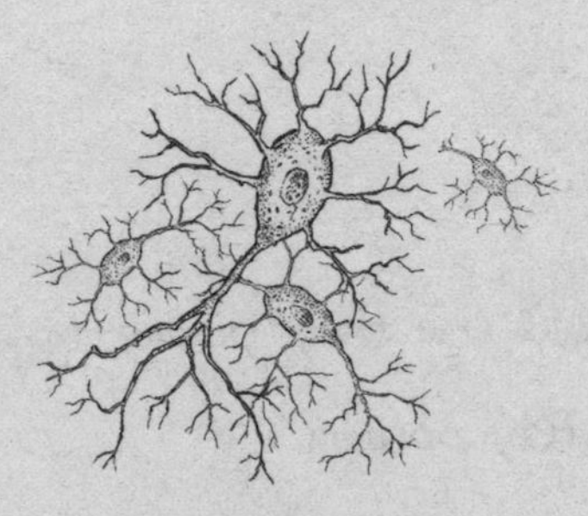

The ability of your brain to change with learning is called neuroplasticity.

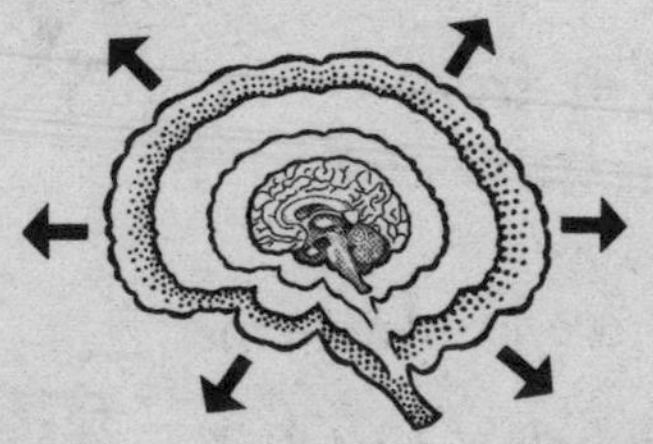

So don't be annoyed if someone teases you about your plastic brain.

That is a pretty amazing feature.

With Michael K. and Agent Umber translating, Major Fluffy quickly explained

- The Anternet
- The E-lephant
- The World Wide Whale

"Eeeek weeek eee eeee weeee eeek eee eke ek ekk ek eee weee."

"'Ants and elephants and whales have had their networks for millions of Earth years. Everyone knows that. But they do not like to be bothered.'"

Michael K. smacked his fist in his palm. "But if they don't help us, it's their world that will disappear too."

"Weee eeek eeek eeek eee. Eeeek eeek eeeeek eeek."

"'So we must contact ants, elephants, and whales.'"

"But how do we do that?" said Umber.

Michael K. pointed to the spaceheadz.com web page.

"Our Spaceheadz. We get everyone who ever signed up to send out the call."

"Eeeeek eeee."

"'Genius.'"

Michael K. quickly built a "spaceheadz.com Red-Hot Action" page and posted it on spaceheadz.com.

Calling All Spaceheadz

We Need Your Help NOW!

We must contact

1. Click a box.

2. Stare at image for 12 seconds.

3. And say out loud:

"Anternet, Anternet, Anternet," or

"E-lephant, E-lephant, E-lephant," or

"World Wide Whale, World Wide Whale,
World Wide Whale."

Agent Umber rubbed his head nervously. "Can our Spaceheadz do it? Will they get the message out in time? Will this work?"

"It better work," said Michael K. "It's our very last chance to save the world."

The bull elephant wrapped his trunk around the red and white stake hammered into the ground.

With one mighty pull he yanked it out of the ground.

The chains on Mom K. and Dad K. were now attached to nothing.

"Glooo glah," Baby K. thanked the elephant.

"Bree breep bree," he trumpeted, and nodded.

"I'm not sure what's going on with these elephants," said Dad K., throwing his chain over his shoulder. "But they look like they know exactly what they are doing."

The bull elephant offered Dad K. his trunk as a step, then lifted Dad K. onto his back.

Another elephant lifted Mom K. and Baby K. gently onto its back.

"It's like they all got a signal or something," said Mom K.

The small herd of elephants and the Family K. rumbled off down the road into the night.

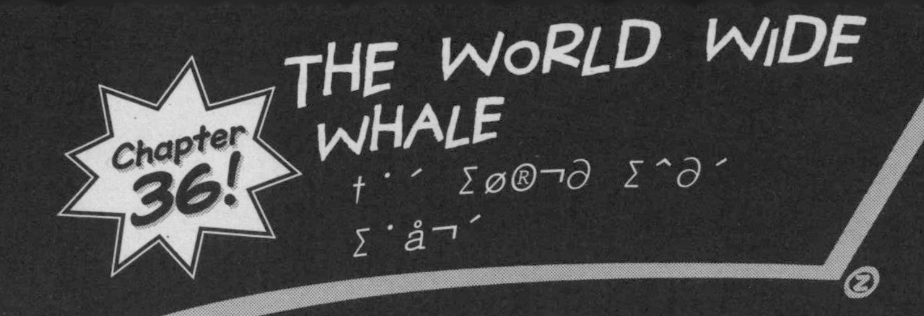

Four enormous black whales with white throats, flippers, and underbelly markings rocketed completely out of the water by the light of the dock.

They landed with a giant smack on the water and a wave of their V-shaped tails.

"Yep," said the old man. "Humpbacks. And they want you to follow them."

A chorus of high-pitched whistles and echoing shrieks vibrated in the cold night air.

"How do you know?" asked Delta.

"They just sang it to me," said the grizzled old man. "That's why I untied you. Now you better get going, pronto. Something big is up."

One of the whales poked its head out of the water not five feet away from the DarkWave X stealth boat and looked them over with its giant eyeball.

"This whale team is on a mission," said Foxtrot. "And we are with them. Full speed ahead, Delta!"

"Aye, aye, skipper," said Delta. And he cranked the engines to catch up with the pod of whales streaking away in the gray Alaskan night.

The whales shrieked and clicked and moaned.

The old man sang to no one but himself:

"Give me some time to blow the man down!"

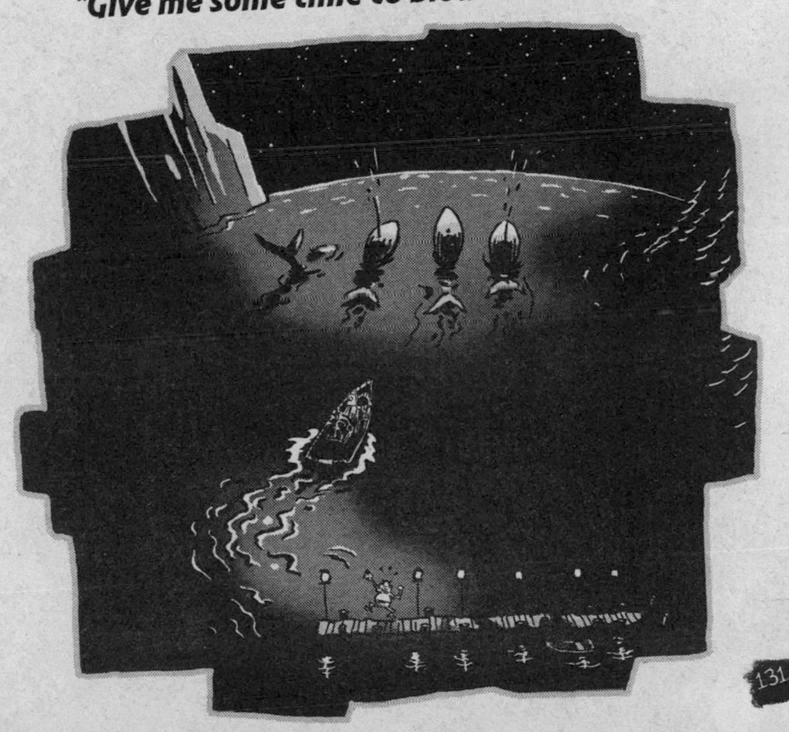

Hot Magenta crouched down on one knee on the trail.

She could not believe what she was seeing.

As an AAA agent, she had seen some pretty strange sights around the world. But this was the strangest sight ever. And she knew it was meant for no one else but her.

There was a sign on the ground.

The sign was in the shape of an arrow pointing north.

And the sign said:

But that wasn't the strange part.

The strange part was that this sign was made entirely of ants. Living ants. Hundreds of thousands of millions of ants. All of them pointing and moving north.

"Okaaaay," said Hot Magenta.

Because what else do you say to an army of ants that has just delivered a message to you?

And she followed the army ants into the night.

Brain III

If you use your brain, it will change and grow by making connections, networks, circles.

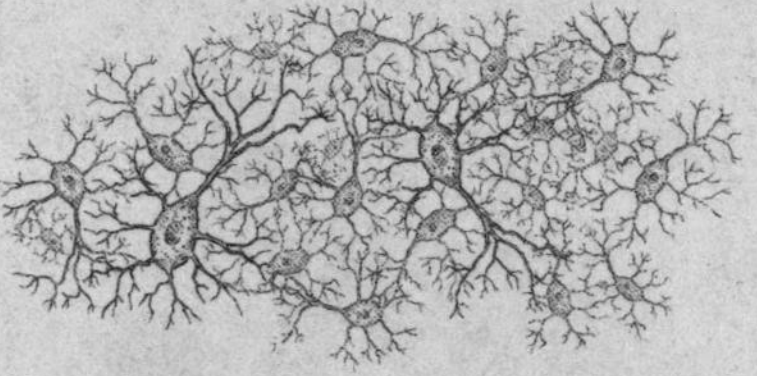

Individual organisms change and grow and improve their chances of survival by making connections, networks, circles.

Use your brain.

Connect with others.

Change and grow.

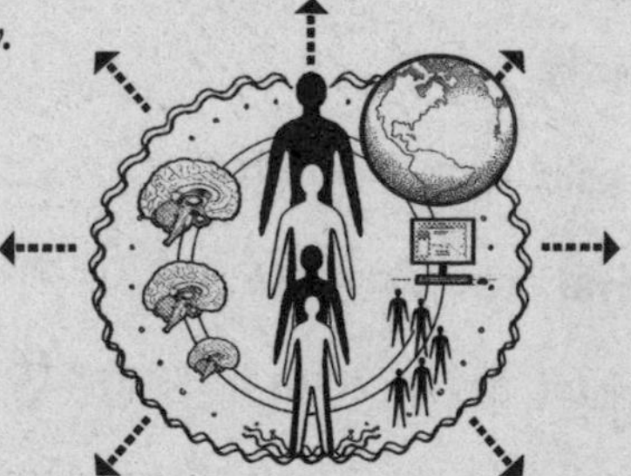

HAPPY? GRADUATION

·åππ¥¿ ©®å∂¨åt^ø˜

"Eeeeeeeeee," squealed the microphone on the wooden platform set up in the yard of P.S. 858.

The crowd of moms and dads and little brothers and sisters sitting on folding chairs sat up and looked to the front.

A banner stretching the length of the platform spelled out in bright, hand-colored letters

A smaller banner stapled to the bottom of the first spelled out in ragged black Magic Marker

"Welcome, welcome, welcome," said the little, bald man at the microphone. "I am the new principal. And I am so excited for our ceremony today!" he said in a high, squeaky voice.

The crowd clapped politely.

A first grader cheered, "Hooray!"

"Yes, 'hooray' indeed," said the chief/principal. "This has been a long time coming. And it is going to be the start of something very big."

The chief stopped and waited until he got more applause.

He was starting to like people applauding him the way they were supposed to.

The chief smiled in the warm spring noontime sun. Then he turned and motioned to the four kids and machinery onstage.

"Today I have with me four special fifth graders from Mrs. Halley's class. They are Venus, TJ, Bob, and Jennifer."

"Hooray!" cheered the first grader again.

"Okay, knock it off, kid," said the chief/principal.

"They aren't even doing anything. They are just standing there."

And that was true.

The four kids next to the big black egg-shaped thing onstage were just standing there, perfectly still.

"These SP—uh . . . I mean, fifth graders are going to help me with our new beginning."

The chief/principal looked up over the crowd, searching for one particular person.

He looked back at the stage and so did not see that particular person, Michael K., skateboard up and hide behind a tree right next to a giant doughnut.

"Because every new beginning starts with an ending," said the chief/principal. "And even though this ending might be tough on some persons, it's going to be very exciting for someone else who has lived on this planet for a very long time and who will now RULE THE UNIVERSE!!!!"

The chief/principal paused.

The crowd clapped even though they had no idea what the chief/principal was talking about.

The chief checked his watch. Then he looked over to the stage again. "You see," he explained, pointing to the giant red ray-gun-shaped thing. "That is a Red-Hot Ray. It is powered by a three point one four million plus one Brainwave."

The crowd murmured. Now they were getting confused. What did this have to do with fifth-grade graduation?

The chief continued, "And I have three point one four million of that Brainwave." The chief pulled out his sparking blue snow globe. "I have it right here. But I need one more something from one fifth grader."

The chief looked out over the crowd.

He still did not see the one fifth grader he was looking for.

Michael K., still hiding behind the tree, looked up and down the street. Nothing. He looked up into the sky. Nothing.

"And if I don't get that one something," said the chief/principal, "I am going to have to change the channel on these four." The chief pulled out what looked like an ordinary TV remote and pointed it at Bob and Jennifer and TJ and Venus. "Their Energy Waves will be rearranged. They will become nothing more than a bad smell."

Now the crowd was completely confused.

"Is this part of the fifth-grade play?" said a mom in a yellow sundress.

"If it is, the principal is a very convincing bad guy," said a dad.

Michael K. looked at the giant doughnut. "We can't let him do this."

The doughnut shook his head. "You can't stop him. We have to wait for the Anternet, the E-lephant, and the World Wide Whale."

"Eeeek eeek," said Major Fluffy.

"It didn't work," said Michael K. to the giant doughnut with the hamster in his pocket standing next to him. "We didn't get to them in time. It's all over."

The chief walked across the stage.

The crowd watched in silence, still thinking this was the strangest graduation ceremony ever.

The first and second graders in the audience started wiggling.

The chief stood in front of Venus, TJ, Bob, and Jennifer. "Any last words, Spacedoofs?"

"**CHOPS AND SLICES!**" said Bob.

"**TONES AND SHAPES!**" said Jennifer.

"**DO THE DEW,**" said TJ.

"**ADVANCED MEDICINE FOR PAIN,**" said Venus.

"Perfect," said the chief. "Brains like mush."

He raised the Wave-Changer remote and—

"Wait!" yelled a voice in the back of the crowd.

The chief paused.

Michael K. ran up the aisle and hopped onstage.

"I can't let you do this to my friends. Let them go. I'll give you my brain wave."

"How nice," said the chief.

"Don't do it, Michael K.!" yelled the giant doughnut in the audience.

"Eeeee eeeeek!" said the hamster in the doughnut's pocket.

"Why is there a doughnut in the play?" asked the mom in the yellow dress.

"I don't know," said the dad. "But he was in the kindergarten play, too. I think he is the school mascot."

"Let my friends go. Take my brain wave. And let's get this over with," said Michael K.

"Finally," said the chief.

"Do it!" said Michael K.

The chief lowered the Wave-Changer remote. He took out the Spaceheadz Brainwave globe.

"All you have to do is click here," said the chief.

AGREE.

"And then it's all over."

Michael K. paused.

He looked all around one last time, hoping to see someone, something, anything, riding to his rescue.

Michael K. saw only confused-looking moms and dads and kids.

He was going to have to do this on his own.

Michael K. clicked on **AGREE**.

Michael K.'s plus-one brain wave sparked into the globe.

The snow globe instantly supercharged to a blinding, powerful electric blue.

The fire button on the Red-Hot Ray lit green and displayed

"Yes!" yelled the chief. "Yes, yes, yes!" He spun around in a little circle. "I have the full Brainwave! I fire the ray, and I am ruler of the universe!"

The graduation crowd applauded politely, hoping this was the end of the strangest graduation performance they had ever seen.

Michael K. hung his head.

He walked over to the IWANT Pulsar and gave it a solid kick, knocking it off the stage. The humming black egg cracked open on the concrete and exploded in a mess of wires and circuit boards.

The WantWaves stopped.

Venus, TJ, Bob, and Jennifer looked around like they had just woken up.

"Michael K.," said Venus. "What is going on?"

"I'll tell you what's going on, Spacesuckers," said the chief. "You are done! Michael K. just handed over the final plus-one brain wave. The Red-Hot Ray is ready to fire. And this is the End."

The chief grabbed the firing handles of the Red-Hot Ray.

"Not one hundred percent natural!' said Bob.

"Not one hundred percent organic!" said Jennifer.

But they were too late.

The chief pulled the triggers.

The Red-Hot Ray unleashed a wave powered by the full 3.14 million plus one Brainwave.

And you would not believe what happened next.

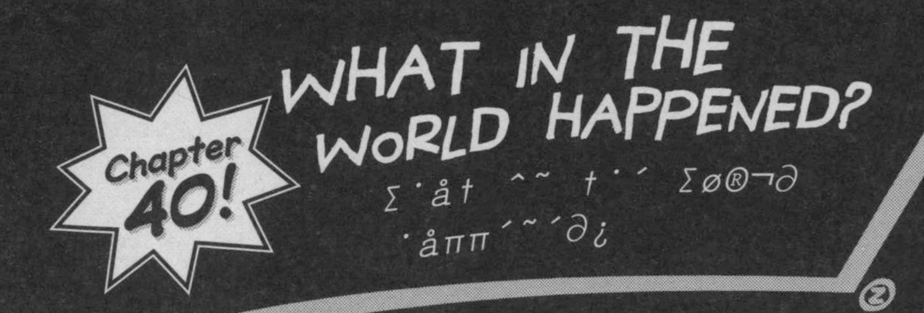

by Willy and Hugo

Willy and Hugo raced into the kitchen, bug-eyed wild and stuck-out-hair crazy.

"Bam!" yelled Willy.

"Kaboom!" yelled Hugo.

They ran into each other and wrestled into a heap on the floor.

"Boys, boys, boys," said Willy's mom. "What are you doing? Did you have fun with your grammy and grampy at the graduation ceremony? What in the world happened?"

Grammy and Grampy walked into the kitchen following Willy and Hugo. They looked a bit bug-eyed and crazy haired too.

Willy and Hugo explained everything.

"The principal made a giant ray gun."

"And he was going to change the kids' channel to make them poof like a bad smell!"

"And then Michael K. said 'I will save you!'"

"And he knocked over the thing!"

"But then the bad guy tricked him."

"And Michael K.'s friends were sad."

"And the giant doughnut."

"And the hamster."

"And then the bad guy shotted the giant gun."

"BRRRRRRRRRRRZZZZZZZZZ!!!!!"

"And he thought he won!"

"But then—"

"BWEEEEEEEE!" said Willy, crawling around on his hands and knees. "Boom, boom, boom, boom."

Hugo scrambled after Willy like a bug. "Ack, ack, ack, ack!"

They both jumped up and started pretending they were floating and flying around the kitchen table, singing, "WEEEEEE-OOOOOOOO, WEEEEEEOOOOO, WEEEEOOOOOO!"

"And then RRRRRRRRRRRRRRrrrrr!"

"And ZZZZZZZZZZZZZzzzzzz!"

Hugo and Willy wrapped their arms around each other and spun in circles.

"Spaceheadz for life!"

"Spaceheadz for life!

"SPACEHEADZ FOR LIFE!"

"SPACEHEADZ FOR LIFE!"

"BAM!"

"KABOOOM!"

The little guys fell on their backs.

"Then he tried to get away!"

"And Michael K. wrestled the principal."

"And sucked him right into the glass ball with a TV changer!"

"So Hooray! SPACEHEADZ FOR LIFE!"

"Wow," said Willy and Hugo's mom. "You boys have the most strange and wonderful imaginations."

Hugo and Willy did have strange and wonderful imaginations.

But for the first time ever, what Willy and Hugo imagined was not as strange or wonderful as what really happened.

What really happened was this:

The chief pulled the triggers. The Red-Hot Ray unleashed the full and almost unbelievable power of 3.14 million plus one brain waves networked together.

Every leaf of every tree in the school yard stood on end. The trees themselves bent backward. The metal folding chairs vibrated and half lifted off the ground, as if they were about to follow the blast up into the sky and off into deep space. The graduation parents and kids hung on for their lives.

"Oh, no!" said Venus. "Planet Gonf is doomed!"

"Oh, yes," said the chief. "And your planet gets turned off next. This is your End. My Beginning!"

"I am having a very hard time following the plot of this graduation play," said a mom.

"The evil principal said this is the End," said a dad. "I think it is a metaphor for destruction and rebirth in change."

The giant doughnut with the hamster in his pocket climbed onstage.

"But why does the doughnut have a hamster?" asked the mom.

"To represent the squeakiness of life?" guessed the dad.

"That makes no sense."

The monster power wave pulsed away from the playground of P.S. 858 into space, bending light, colors, and time.

Michael K. fell on his hands and knees.

"Too late . . ."

Bob and Jennifer stared up into the sky.

"Nothing can stop me now!" yelled the chief.

But he was so wrong.

Because just then the ground shook. The air itself throbbed with a beat so low it was not heard, but felt.

"BWEEEEE BWEEEE!" came a sound.

Michael K. looked up

"Eeek wee eeek eeek," said Major Fluffy.

And he was so right.

Because sure enough, two seconds later, an entire herd of elephants pounded down the streets on either side of P.S. 858. Broad gray ears flapping, trunks swaying, the elephants stormed into the playground and surrounded the stage. A mom clown and a baby clown waved from the top of the lead elephant. A dad clown with giant green shoes waved from another.

The elephants rocked and boomed their subsonic pulses in unison.

The graduation crowd liked this new addition to the ceremony/play. They clapped and cheered.

The chief looked a little freaked out. "So you contacted the E-lephant network. Big deal. You will need more than that."

And at exactly that moment a dark red swarm of color welled up over the back of the stage and swirled around the Red-Hot Ray.

"Ants!" said kindergartner Hugo, because he had just read about them in his science book. "Army ants!"

And Hugo was right.

Army ants, millions of them, swarmed up and over the Red-Hot Ray. Up and all over the surrounding trees. A lady dressed like a scientific explorer climbed onstage with the ants and hugged the doughnut.

"Ha!" yelled the chief. "The Anternet. So what? My Red-Hot Ray is still more powerful than your networks combined!"

And that was also exactly right . . . at least until the whales showed up.

Because that is what happened next: The whales showed up.

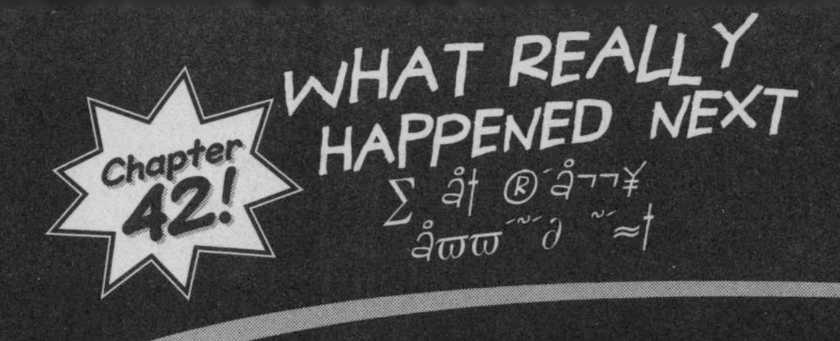

"Wait a minute," said a third grader in the graduation audience, saying exactly what you are thinking. "Whales can't just show up over a school playground in the middle of Brooklyn."

"Then what are those?" said the third grader's best friend, pointing to the crowd of whales drifting above the P.S. 858 playground like huge black clouds with streaks of white in the bright blue sky.

"Bweeeeoooooooo weeeeeeeoooooooooo weeeeooo weee we weeee wwoooo," sang the whales.

The whales floated like giant living zeppelins. They were powered by unlikely, but not impossible, forces made by linking nerve cell energy to repel gravitational forces and amplify both solar and sonar energy . . . understood by no one at the P.S. 858 graduation except Jennifer.

"The World Wide Whale?" said the chief, now looking a bit more panicked.

"The World Wide Whale," said Michael K. "And we networked everyone together with our very own spaceheadz.com."

"Wee eeek eeek eee eee. Eeeek eeekeee weee eee eeeek," said Major Fluffy.

"Of course," said Bob.

"***STRONGER THAN DIRT!***" said Jennifer.

Michael K. waved to his mom and dad and baby sister on the elephants.

The elephants thrummed, "Whooom whooom whooom."

Michael K. gave the thumbs-up sign to Agent Hot Magenta.

The ants clicked and tapped, "Klaaak klaaak klaaak."

Michael K. saluted overhead to the DarkWave X agents and their whales.

The whales sang, "Bweooooo weoooo weoooo."

The chief grabbed the handles of his Red-Hot Ray and aimed the power wave at the floating whales.

Michael K. dived across the stage, tackled the chief, and knocked him to the ground.

The Red-Hot Ray blast spun wildly in the sky.

The triple elephant/whale/ant wave grew and swelled alongside the wave still streaming from the Red-Hot Ray.

Bob grabbed the graduation microphone and started chanting, "SPHDZ for life, SPHDZ for life, SPHDZ for life . . ."

TJ, Venus, and Jennifer joined in. "Spaceheadz for life, Spaceheadz for life, Spaceheadz for life . . ."

The elephants stamped in time.

The ants bobbed and clicked.

The whales swirled in midair circles.

The triple wave grew larger and stronger.

The graduation crowd added their voices: "Spaceheadz for life, Spaceheadz for life, Spaceheadz for life . . ."

"Nooooooooo!" yelled the chief, struggling in Michael K.'s headlock.

The Spaceheadz for life wave snaked around and through the chief's Red-Hot Ray wave.

Waves collided and canceled.

Waves built and grew.

The earth itself seemed to slow and shake for a minute, and then . . .

BAM!

KABOOM!

A flash so bright everything went white.

Just before everything went black.

"This just in at our Channel Four News Center," said the man in the suit coat on TV. "A huge beam of energy was tracked coming out of New York City today.

"Scientists first thought it was a solar flare.

"But they quickly determined that the energy beam was moving away from Earth.

"And then, stranger still, an even larger beam formed. . . .

"It intercepted the first beam . . .

"And scattered both beams in a massive *bam!* and *kaboom!* that spelled out this mysterious message across the stratosphere:

"Scientists are now saying they have absolutely no idea what this was. But it's gone now. So don't worry."

The man in the suit coat shuffled his papers.

"In other news—residents of Brooklyn have been calling in sightings of a herd of elephants, a swarm of army ants, and a pod of whales. Now, that is just not possible. So we are not reporting that."

Chapter 44! MISSION ACCOMPLISHED?

µ^ßß^ø~
åççøµπ¬^ß˙´∂¿

Michael K. sat at his desk in room 501-B of P.S. 858. Right where it all started. And now right where it was all ending.

They were all Spaceheadz now.

Bob packed his My Little Pony collection into his Dora the Explorer backpack. Jennifer gathered up a backpack full of her favorite-flavored colored pencils. Major Fluffy took one more spin on his hamster wheel.

Venus, messing with her laptop as usual, called up www.imsuregladthatdidnthappen.com.

She typed in the password: CHIEF PRINCIPAL.

She and TJ watched the waves from the Red-Hot Ray cover Gonf and then . . .

"Yikes," said TJ.

"You can say that again," said Venus.

"Yikes," said Bob.

Venus and TJ laughed.

Mrs. Halley took down the last of her dog decorations from the bulletin board. "I'm so glad to see you kids one more time before we all disappear."

"The Spaceheadz are leaving," said Michael K. "They wanted to pack up a few supplies to take back to their planet . . . I mean, country."

Michael K. handed Mrs. Halley a black poodle.

"That's so nice," said Mrs. Halley. "I'm sure they will be very happy to get back to Bulgaria. It's been quite a year."

Michael K. thought about correcting Mrs. Halley, explaining the Spaceheadz, their planet, and their crazy mission. "Yes," he said. "Yes, it has."

"And I am going to be happy to get to my retirement spot. It's a wonderfully quiet spot in Nevada. With a very simple address to remember: Area Fifty-one."

"Squeee eerea eee ee ee?" said Major Fluffy.

"Perfect," said Venus.

"News from HQ!" said Jennifer, holding up her Nintendo Game Boy communicator.

The screen flashed:

Congratulations, SPHDZ.

MISSION SUCCESS!

The Game Boy burst into the Super Mario Bros. song.

"And even more free range!" said Bob.

The screen flashed:

Your SPHDZ 4 LIFE wave reached home planet.
General Accounting was instantly channel-changed.
New commander: GENERAL FLUFFY!

More of the Super Mario Bros. song bleeped and blooped.

Michael K. smiled. "You have got to be—"

"BEEEEEEEEP!" interrupted the classroom loudspeaker. "Michael K. and Spaceheadz Bob, Jennifer, and Fluffy report to the principal's office immediately," said the voice of the school nurse.

And before anyone could freak out or ask questions, Nurse Dominique added, "You have a visitor. Level Gold Red."

Chapter 45! HAIL TO THE CHIEF(S)

·å^¬ tø t·´

ç·^´ƒ (ß)

Michael K., Venus, and TJ walked the empty halls of P.S. 858 with their Spaceheadz pals.

"What the heck is Level Gold Red?" said Venus.

"Very top," said Bob.

"Extra-hot," said Jennifer.

"Eeeee squeee," said General Fluffy.

Nurse Dominique met them at the door to the main office. She squeezed everyone into one of her giant hugs.

"We are so proud of all of you," said Nurse D.

Michael K. realized Nurse D. knew a lot more than he had ever thought she did.

"Now, look sharp. Come on, come on. You've got special people waiting on you."

Nurse D. hustled them through the office and into the principal's office.

With the lights off and the shades down, Michael K. and the Spaceheadz couldn't see much more than the outline of three shapes behind the desk.

"Michael K.," said a deep voice. "You are a hero to your school, your country, and your planet. Because this is such a sensitive matter, with kids and hamsters and what have you from other worlds, we cannot let the public know about this. But I did want to give you my official presidential congratulations."

The tall shadow in the middle extended his hand.

Michael K. shook it. And he could have sworn the guy had just said "presidential congratulations."

"This will not go on public record, but your mom and dad and baby sister are now Top Clearance ZIA. Team DarkWave X will head the new NNA—Natural Networks Agency. And the new head of the AAA and I would also like to present you with something . . . and ask you for a bit of help."

Michael K.'s eyes adjusted to the dim light. He saw

a woman with long blond hair step around the desk, followed by a giant taco.

"Agent Umber? You are the new head of the AAA?"

The giant taco laughed. "No way. I would never want that job. I am just a giant taco," said the giant taco. "Here is the new head of the AAA."

Agent Hot Magenta stepped forward and pinned small silver Earth pins on Venus, TJ, Bob, and Jennifer. She tucked one into Fluffy's paw.

"For your good works in protecting and serving—"

"And always looking up," added the giant taco.

"You are now lifetime agents of the AAA," said Chief Hot Magenta. She pulled out a familiar snow globe. Except now, instead of being filled with the blue sparking Spaceheadz Brainwave, it held the one small, angry red pulse that used to be the chief, pinging off the sides like mad.

"And we will need your help. We need you to keep your Spaceheadz for Life network powered up, and to keep this bad Spaceheadz in his place. Can you do that?"

"Yes, sir," answered Venus. "We are all Spaceheadz for life."

Nurse Dominique took the globe. "Oh, I got a spot on my desk for this bad energy."

"Thank you, Chief Hot Magenta," added Venus. "But it's a little awkward being Anti-Alien agents. We really like our alien pals."

"Take a look at your AAA card," said Chief Hot Magenta with a smile.

Venus read her new AAA card aloud: "'AAA—the Alien Assistance Agency.' Perfect."

"And Michael K.," said the president—because yes, it really was the president—standing up to go. "You may choose any branch of service you want. Any title or job is yours. You saved the world. You really can do anything. Just let me know what it is you choose."

Michael K. didn't know what to say.

"And let me also say," continued the president, "I hereby officially graduate all of you to sixth grade."

And then the president was out the door and out of school like he had never been there.

Michael K. and Venus and TJ stood on the empty playground facing Bob and Jennifer.

The wrecked IWANT Pulsar sat in the trash by the monkey bars.

Bob held General Fluffy.

Jennifer held the Spaceheadz Wave-Changer remote.

Michael K. wasn't quite sure what you say to friends who are headed off to another planet. Good-bye? Good warp? Good luck?

Venus gave everyone a hug.

So TJ and Michael K. did the same.

Michael K. was sad to see his pals from another planet go. But he was also kind of glad. They were a lot of work. But at least maybe he had helped them learn something about the power of their own minds.

"Stay ultrafresh," said Bob, waving.

"Stay ultrasoft," said Jennifer, showing her extra roll of Charmin toilet paper.

Or maybe not.

"Eeee eeek," said General Fluffy. He gave one final salute.

"SPHDZ 4 life!'" translated both Bob and Jennifer.

Jennifer pressed the change channel button on the Spaceheadz remote.

The shapes of Bob, Jennifer, and Fluffy blurred, scrambled into balls of energy, and winked out.

Michael K., Venus, and TJ stared at the empty spot at the bottom of the playground slide where the Spaceheadz had just been standing.

"Well, that was not very impressive," said Venus.

"Would have been cooler if they had a really nice saucer or spaceship," said TJ.

"Wow," said Michael K.

He felt kind of empty, a little bit disconnected.

Venus gave him a soft punch in the arm.

"Nice work, Michael K. You saved the world. Now what are you going to do?"

Michael K. looked up into the sky. He couldn't see any stars or planets. But he knew they were up there and out there.

Michael K. thought about all of the Spaceheadz craziness of the last year.

Michael K. thought about networks and connections, webs and circles, herds and flocks, enemies and friends.

The smallest electrical pulse fired across a complicated network of Michael K.'s brain cells.

This pulse produced a thought.

"You know what I'm going to do?" said Michael K. "First I'm going to have a great summer vacation."

Michael K. looked at Venus and TJ, his real friends.

"And then I am going to take on the hardest job. I'm going to be a sixth grader."

The ants marched.

The elephants trumpeted.

The whales sang.

And for the first time in a long time, the earth turned peacefully in its orbit, protected by its always-growing network of connected

"SPHDZ 4 life!"